WORTH MORE DEAD

SHANON L. MAYER

# WORTH MORE DEAD

## SHADOW TRIBUNAL, BOOK 2

Shanon Mayer

First Printing, 2024

Cover design by JD&J Design
ISBN: 978-1-958076-23-1, 978-1-958076-24-8, 978-1-958076-26-2
Published by Shanon L. Mayer, Vancouver WA 98663
https://shanonlmayer.com

# BOOKS BY SHANON L. MAYER

Chronicles of the Chosen
Sphere of Power
Veil of Deception
Reflections of Doubt
Palace of Stone

Jen Rice
Captives and Prisoners
Festival of Souls
Beautiful Monsters
Mind Games

Inland Sea
Star of Darkness
Eyes of Midnight
Grand Coven

Shadow Tribunal
Diamond Queen
Worth More Dead

For you. You know who you are.

# WAKING UP DEAD

The air was thick and heavy, smothering in the blackness that surrounded M'Tarl. Not only that, but there was a mossy, earthy scent that she couldn't quite figure out. As she slowly came to consciousness, she realized that it wasn't just the air that was thick and heavy, there was something pressing tightly around her. It seemed like almost every inch of her body was restrained somehow, which was not a feeling she enjoyed even on the best of days. Only the smallest pocket of air had granted her enough room to continue breathing, air that was quickly thinning and running low. Confused and uncertain of how she had arrived in this strange situation, she tried to look around, but the dirt held her tightly.

"Buried?" she asked herself quietly as she determined how bad of a situation she was in. She spat out a mouthful of dirt, realizing that opening her mouth while underground probably wasn't the wisest of decisions. "That's a new one for me, I haven't been buried before. I guess I should just be thankful they hadn't chosen a more creative method of body disposal." She reached out with her senses, confused when she got nothing in return. Not even the slightest trace of life filtered through her mind, something she had never experienced before except in the furthest reaches of space. Her breathing quickened slightly as she tried to reach out again, and then again, with similar results. All she got was the same nothing she had gotten the first time.

Even as she strained to detect something, her mind turned to probable situations in which she might currently find herself. Her absolute worst-case situation but, given the lack of psionic response was the most likely one, was that she had been encased in a box of dirt and then jettisoned out into space. If that was the case, then she was dead regardless of what actions she may take. Since that option had no hope of survival, she decided there was no point in worrying about it and instead turned her attention to the more survivable, if less likely, options before her. She had to be either in the same dirt-filled box that she had just imagined floating around in space, only this time within the confines of a planet, or had been buried, coffin-less, underground. Of the possibilities, she liked the idea of having been buried without a coffin the most, as it had the highest chance of survival.

She just hoped that she had been buried neither too deep nor under something solid, because the meager air pocket she had avail-able wouldn't last for much longer. Realizing that she was still breathing quickly, she slowed herself down, willing herself to calm. She needed to think rationally, and panicking had no place in her escape plans.

If panicking became a necessity, she could do that later, once she was safe.

Since she had been unconscious when placed into this particular position, she had no clue how long she had been in it, but she was thankful that at the very least she had woken before the air was depleted entirely. As she began to dig her way out, her entire body began to scream in pain, causing her to stop every so often to rest but she had no time to relax. Just as she had no time to panic, she had no time to whine about a little bit of pain.

Even if it was a substantial amount more than just a little bit.

If she didn't reach the air soon, the grave would become permanent. Just the movements she had already made had caused the air pocket to collapse under the moving dirt. She gritted her teeth and continued to dig, holding her breath and pushing aside the pain that persistently screamed through her body. She would figure out why she hurt so much later, once she was in a position to breathe freely again.

Three minutes later, she reached the surface and took in a deep breath of clear air, coughing out some loose grains of soil that had found themselves in places they didn't belong. Only the rigorous training she had undergone early in her career had allowed her to remain calm during her escape, as moving while suffocating would have induced immediate panic in most people. She, on the other hand, was hardly like most people. After a few more breaths, she took a look around to figure out not only where she was but also where to go from there.

It was still far too early to panic. The pain, on the other hand, was quickly growing to be more than just a simple annoyance.

She was in an area thick with trees and no sounds of life nearby. After pulling herself the rest of the way out of the ground, she lay on the grass next to her grave, enjoying the presence of fresh air. The memories of all that had transpired leading up to her untimely burial and thoughts of those who believed her dead flickered through her mind, but she shoved them aside. She had more important things to attend to than to search for people who were certainly long gone. After all, this wasn't the first time M'Tarl had been left for dead and, given her career, it was unlikely to be the last.

Briefly very concerned, she tapped her chest, relieved to discover that her most precious item, the small silvery ring that had been her constant companion since childhood, was still hanging by its chain in place around her neck. Had anything happened to that trinket, she would have been in a much less benevolent mood.

She reached out with her senses to find the closest inhabited area and frowned in confusion when she found the same nothing she had identified while still buried. There were no detectable thought patterns within her radius of effect, which meant that either she was much further away from civilization than she had first realized or there was something substantially wrong. Her psionics had never failed her before and she wondered what her captors had done to her once she had lost consciousness for them to cease working in this way. She had attributed her previous failure when trying to sense where she was to the moderately-well-contained panic at having been buried alive, but she was no longer convinced that was the case.

For starters, she was no longer buried, underground or otherwise. The pressure she had felt from the dirt packed around her was gone as well, which had thankfully helped to reduce the amount of pain she was in. Movement still caused her to hiss but she could still function. She wasn't quite dead and intended to stay that way for as long as possible.

Glancing around, she appreciated the serenity of the clearing in which she had been buried. "At least you picked a nice spot for me," she conceded. "Might have been nice had you waited just a little longer before putting me here, though." She winced again as she pushed herself to her feet, wondering how extensive the damage was. Covered in earth as she was, she wouldn't be able to see the extent of the damage until a substantial cleaning effort, so she didn't bother trying a thorough evaluation.

With a little luck, there would be a stream or other source of clear water nearby that she could use to cleanse her wounds and stave off at least some of the infection that she was sure had already begun to spread throughout her body. Dirt, for all its benefits, was hardly the optimal poultice for open wounds. Staying put wasn't an option, so she had no other choice. She picked a direction and began to walk. She stumbled only a few times, sore muscles and open wounds protesting loudly against the forced march, but she ignored all of it.

The sun was beginning to glint from the treetops an hour later, an orange glow washing over the horizon as the skies turned pink and blue, indicating the advent of sunrise, when M'Tarl spotted the edge of a town. She reached out her senses again, knowing for certain that someone had to be within her range, but still received no information in return. Her brows furrowed in frustration. She could see visually that there were people waking and heading out into their morning business, but she couldn't hear a single thought from any of them. Either these people had suddenly gained some sort of psychic defenses that they hadn't possessed the previous day or there was something else blocking her from hearing them.

The thought that none of this was going according to plan fluttered through her mind and she chuckled at herself at the understatement of it all. Not only was she not supposed to have been almost killed, but she also definitely wasn't supposed to have lost her abilities while doing so. This, she was certain, was the very definition of something going wrong.

Thankfully, she recognized the town. She had personally landed her ship just beyond the sleepy little residential area so as long as it was still there, clean water and bandages awaited her. There was nothing more for her to do in the area, so she made short time moving past the houses and other assorted buildings to reach the parking area. A handful of the residents watched her with open curiosity as she passed, for which she hardly blamed them. Half-dead people who appeared to have recently crawled out of their own graves were probably not everyday occurrences there.

If they were, she chuckled to herself, then the town had much more important problems to contend with than one lone Qadar.

"Are you okay, miss?" One young woman stepped forward, concern and apprehension playing across her face. "You don't look so good."

"Thank you, I appreciate the concern, but I'll be fine," M'Tarl smiled in return. "It's just been a long night." Without being able to read the woman's thoughts, it was impossible to tell whether she was as charitable as she appeared and M'Tarl was in no mood to take unnecessary chances.

Her ship, a small cruiser, waited exactly where she had left it, a great relief. Part of her mind had been convinced that the people who had buried her had also taken possession of it, leaving her without easy egress from the area. While she harbored no ill will towards the townspeople, she had little interest in remaining planetside any longer than necessary, at least on that particular planet. Should her would-be murderers discover her empty grave, they would certainly come in search of her, and she intended to be as far away as possible before that could happen. Even more so now since she couldn't sense them coming. Being blindsided was not a prospect to which she was used, and she had no intention of giving anyone such an advantage, particularly those who wished her dead.

The first thing she did after powering the ship on was to engage the active camouflage, unwilling to draw any further attention to herself during takeoff. Although small craft such as hers were common in the skies above, an observant onlooker may notice her departure, which was also low on her list of things she wanted to happen. The autopilot engaged as soon as she was in orbit and she set the destination to the last planet she had been on where she knew she would be safe.

# LOVAN SPACE

Steam showers were the single greatest invention in the history of the galaxy, of that M'Tarl was absolutely positive. Running water likely would have hurt as it pounded against her tender flesh, but steam was a gentle and much-needed caress of warmth and cleanliness. After setting her course, she let the autopilot to do its business and headed to get herself cleaned up and determine the extent of the damage.

Her body was practically covered with wounds and injuries everywhere she could see, which dulled her skin to more of a faded tan than the bright golden color it normally was. Puncture wounds covered her abdomen and chest, caused by the long, sharpened blade that had been slowly and not very kindly pushed under her flesh. None of the stabs were deep enough to puncture her internal organs, less by accident and more by design. When being interrogated using such measures, death is usually not the end goal. Keeping one's prisoner alive until the information was gleaned was far more desirable. Bruises marked the areas between the punctures and a series of tiny pinprick dots traced a path up and down both of her arms from the needle-spiked wheel they had used during that portion of her questioning. That wheel had been new, one she hadn't encountered before, and she didn't particularly like it. Space that wasn't colored by punctures and bruises was heavily abraded, both from the implements used against her and, she suspected, from being dragged to her burial site. Some, she supposed, were also from her escape from that same burial plot.

"What's this?" she asked as she pulled a tiny sliver of metal from one of the tiny but painful holes. "Looks like your little toy wasn't as sturdy as you thought it was." She spent the next while going over every inch of skin she could see, examining every injury for more leftover remnants. She plucked a few slivers from beneath her skin, similar to the first she had found, but didn't uncover anything that she found too concerning. A few tiny shards of metal were hardly life-threatening. Assuming, of course, that the metallic flakes were standard metals and not something toxic to the body.

She knew that she should be in a more pain than she was. When the torture had first begun, she had intentionally deadened all of the nerves in her body so that she wouldn't feel the pain as intensely and thus reveal the information her interrogators had been after.

It was standard practice for those who knew how to do it and were in a line of work that required such knowledge. Now, she wasn't sure whether the lack of pain was due to residual deadening from her own defensive efforts or if the injuries she had sustained had caused lasting damage to the nerves themselves.

She winced slightly, more a reflex action than actual pain as her right arm refused to move high enough to scrub the mud from her auburn hair. Her pointed ears, slightly shorter than the tall tips of her race, poked out through the damp mass. Using her left arm to wash her hair was difficult and took much longer than it would have had she maintained use of both arms but she managed. Even if her hair wasn't perfectly clean, it was much better than it had been before the shower. Stepping out onto the small towel placed on the floor to catch any wayward drips, she reached for a second towel to wrap around herself and wiped the fog off of the mirror to get a better look.

She stood slightly under five feet in height, average for a female Qadar. Her cerulean eyes were clear and bright behind the bruised eye sockets. Both of her pupils were the same size, a relief. At least she didn't have a concussion, not that it would have mattered. She opened her mouth and examined their dental work as well, visually confirming what her tongue had already informed her, that one of her teeth had been chipped. She wasn't certain precisely how that particular damage had been done, but that could be repaired easily enough. It wasn't the first time she had needed a replacement tooth. By the time she retired, she would probably have a full mouth of teeth that hadn't originally belonged to her.

"Approaching destination," the autopilot notified her through the ship's communication system. "Anticipated arrival in thirty minutes."

M'Tarl didn't have much more time to waste in the shower. Since Lovus housed a massive military, easily the most widespread fighting force across the galaxy, there were safeguards in place to ensure that access to the planet's airspace was limited to those who were authorized for entry, of which she was not. She stepped into a clean white robe with blue piping along the edges and headed for the bridge, towel in hand to continue drying her hair. There, she discovered she had arrived just in time because as she pulled to a stop, her instruments indicated she was only barely still outside Lovan space.

"State your name and business," an unfamiliar voice demanded over her comms.

"M'Tarl Nox," she responded. "I am in need of medical attention."

"How many aboard?"

"One, it's just me."

"What is the nature of the injury you are seeking treatment for?"

"Superficial, mostly, but there are some puncture wounds that may need attention and the wounds may be infected." After a moment of thought, she added, "There may be possible brain damage involved as well. My psionics aren't working."

There was a pause at the other end. "You

said you're having a problem with your psionic abilities?"

"That's correct. I'm a class two psionist."

Rather than another verbal response, the red warning panel on her instruments changed to green and yellow characters, indicating that she had been cleared a flight path onto the surface of the planet. "Looks like I'm going to Midway General."

Midway General was unarguably the best hospital in the entire galaxy and as such was a desired location for all types of injuries. Since the hospital itself had originally been created to treat all manner of damage caused to the Triad military force, there were specialists on staff for every race and damage type. In fact, it was one of only three hospitals that she knew of that had an entire section of the hospital dedicated to psionic damage. Thankfully, it was no longer restricted to Triad personnel only so people like M'Tarl could gain the advantage of military medical technology.

At least, to some of it. There were things

that even she wasn't able to get her hands onto quite yet.

She was met at the landing strip and directed to park off to the side of the building, yet another vehicle in a row of small space craft such as hers. After powering everything down and setting her security protocols, not that she expected much trouble in the hospital parking lot, she deboarded and walked over to the hospital entrance. Briefly, she wondered whether she should have put on more clothing than just the bathrobe but decided it didn't matter. Every hospital she had ever been to had required changing into their own gowns so by not getting dressed, she was cutting out a rather uncomfortable step in the process.

She did, however, maintain enough presence of mind to grab a set of clothes to dress in when she was done at the hospital. While she had no objections to arriving in just a bathrobe, she fully expected to have the ability to dress herself comfortably when it came time to leave again.

Three medical personnel in powder blue

scrubs met her just inside the doors. "M'Tarl Nox?" A young man with light blond hair pushed a wheelchair towards her, not even bothering to wait for an answer. "I'm Dr. Aditi." He guided her into the seat and began wheeling her down the cold, sterile hallway and into an empty room. The wheels of the chair squeaked slightly as they moved, a surprisingly comforting sound. She had already identified herself as a psionist, so it was no surprise that she had been taken to the specialty wing. The room she had been assigned was large enough, far larger than some of the so-called clinics she had been treated at in the past, with cupboards along two walls, a soft-looking bed complete with a pair of pillows, sheets, and even a blanket. Monitors, each of which had been powered down, were placed off to the side along the third wall of the room, within reach of the bed in case they were needed but far enough aside to be out of the way when they were not.

The best part, in her opinion, is that the room both appeared and smelled clean, a far sight better than the last medical center she had been in.

"What happened to you?" Dr. Aditi finally asked as he helped her settle into the bed.

"Long story," she replied grudgingly, "one I'd rather not tell." She pulled the sleeves of her robe up on her arms to display the wounds there. "There's more on the rest of my body too, I just need to make sure they're not infected."

As he proceeded with his examination, the young doctor looked at her sympathetically. "It looks to me like you were tortured."

"Something like that, yeah."

"And you're a psionist?" When she nodded in response, he made an additional notation in her chart. "I'd like to have more tests done, just to make sure that there isn't something more serious going on or internal damage that you weren't aware of."

"Probably for the best. I can't actually feel any of these right now."

That remark caused an eyebrow to raise. "All of this damage and you don't feel any of it?"

She shook her head. "It hurt quite a lot a few hours ago, when I first woke up, but nothing since I got back to my ship unless I poke at them. I'm not complaining but I'm a little worried that it's going to hurt a lot more later. And I can't lift my arm up very high." She tried to lift her arm to demonstrate her reduced mobility and the doctor made more notes in her chart.

"What has me really concerned, though, is that my psionics don't seem to be working anymore." She explained about waking up in her makeshift gravesite and not being able to sense anything, even after visually identifying people she should have been able to sense easily. "That was when I felt the pain but somewhere between getting out of the ground and getting to my ship the pain went away."

"That definitely calls for more tests," he agreed. "I'm a bit concerned about nerve damage, just as it seems you are. Hopefully it turns out to be nothing too severe. But I've never even heard of someone losing their abilities like that, so I don't know what could have caused that, outside of major brain damage. That will require a bit more effort to find a solution for."

That had been M'Tarl's greatest fear as well. She immediately signed all of the consent forms required to do special scans of her brain to check her psionic function. None of the listed tests were a surprise, as most of them were ones she routinely had done as a part of her employment. Thankfully, none of them were invasive. Those, she suspected, would come later if they weren't able to uncover the source of her problem with surface-level scans.

She really hoped that a biopsy wouldn't be required. She really didn't like biopsies.

"There's a surprising amount of activity here," Dr. Aditi looked up from her brain scans to meet M'Tarl's eyes. He turned the monitor so she could see it as well. "I'm seeing a lot of activity in the area that indicates psioinic abilities." As he spoke, he indicated a section of the image on the screen which showed spikes and valleys, similar to those of a heartbeat.

"That makes sense," she replied. "I'm a psionist."

Dr. Aditi nodded. "I know. But normally if someone was unable to use their abilities, we would see a substantial diminishing in this area." He zoomed in and traced the image of her brain with a pen as he spoke, indicating the area to which he was referring. "I can even see latent scans ongoing here, probably ones you don't consciously use that just happen automatically. Yours look like everything is in tip-top shape, so I'm not sure why your psionics aren't working."

She furrowed her brows at the news. She had figured that the specialists at Midway General would have a quick solution to her problem. The doctor's statements indicated nothing of the sort.

Seeing her expression, Dr. Aditi was quick to add, "there are other tests we can run, of course. There are a number of other things we can do, see if there's a way to elicit some sort of response.

"In the meantime," he pushed away from

the desk and the image under question, his wheeled stool gliding easily across the smooth floor, "let's see what we can do about this surface damage of yours." He called in a couple of assistants, who helped as he worked on treating the wounds that covered the rest of her body.

"I haven't seen damage like this in a long time," he commented finally. M'Tarl wasn't surprised, the obvious signs of a torturous interrogation such as hers were not often seen outside of A.T. space. Given the recent treaty accords, which were still underway as far as she understood, it was highly unlikely that they would be getting any more anytime soon, either. "None of these appear to have become too badly infected," he said at last, to her great relief. "Simple antibiotic treatments should take care of the rest."

"What were they looking for?" One of Dr. Aldi's assistants, a petite nurse with teal hair, inquired.

"I wouldn't tell the people who did all this," M'Tarl responded, gesturing at her skin, "so if I was unwilling to disclose any information under torture, why would I disclose anything under casual conversation?" Although she had no reason to believe that the nurse had anything to do with the group that had recently interrogated her, she wasn't in the habit of revealing any more information, regardless of how inconsequential it may seem, than absolutely necessary. She raised a single eyebrow at the question as though to accentuate her point.

Dr. Aldi and the other doctors at Midway General, talented as they were, healed much of the damage that covered her body from the interrogation but after running every test they could think of, they finally had to admit that they were unable to repair the psionic blockages. The invasive tests that M'Tarl had been concerned about had proven unnecessary, as Dr. Aditi admitted that they would do no good. "Since you show signs of activity in that section of your brain, there's no reason to dig inside to see where the blockage is," he explained when she questioned him on it.

"We've never seen anything like this," the young doctor said as he explained their results, "but I'll definitely keep an ear out. If someone anywhere comes across anything like this, I'll know about it immediately and you'll be the first person I call." He prescribed her an anti-biotic and a healing salve to reduce the scarring, to be applied daily. "Depending on how well this salve does on the scars, you may or may not need additional treatments to remove them. And do remember to be careful. The tissues have been closed but they haven't fully knit together yet. If you do anything too strenuous too quickly, they can re-open"

With nothing further to do, M'Tarl filled out all of the required discharge papers and headed back for her ship. She still had work to do and the lengthy period of time she had spent in the hospital on Lovus had put her behind schedule.

# THE VOIVODE COUNCIL

Her recovery complete, at least to the extent that she could continue her travels safely, M'Tarl waited her turn to leave atmosphere. She had already set her coordinates for Onoquoi, her home planet, but she needed to be outside Lovan space before she could activate the spatial compression drive, the special engine that allowed her ship to travel the enormous distances between star systems almost instantaneously. While she understood the mechanics behind how the drive worked, something about compressing space in front of the ship and expanding the space behind, the minutiae about how it all happened was of little importance to her. All she needed to know was that she had enough fuel to get where she needed to go and whether the blasted thing actually turned on when she needed it to. One of her previous ships had contained a refurbished spatial compression drive that had only worked for about half of the journey, leaving her stranded halfway across the galaxy for over a month. Never again would she buy anything but brand-new, at least as far as drives were concerned. The rest, her autopilot was more than capable of managing with little input from her.

It had been some time since she had been to Onoquoi. While she was technically required to check in with the authorities there no less often than once each month, her assignments often required her to continue in silence for extended periods of time, with even longer absences between appearances before the administration. Her most recent assignment had been no different. As a result, it had been almost two years since her last personal appearance on the planet.

Her turn to exit the atmosphere finally arrived and she let out a sigh of relief. Business must be slow on Lovus today, she realized. If things were heated up, as they so often were, military transports would have taken up every available lane and lower-priority ships such as hers would simply have to wait for a lull in the action. Treaty agreements with A.T. must still be progressing well, otherwise there would be a lot more troop activity. On other planets, she could occasionally use her credentials with the Onoquoi government to expedite things, but Lovus was a different story entirely. Since that planet housed Triad, the galaxy's primary military force, they automatically took priority over everything, other governments be damned. She glanced over at the section of her control panel and scowled. Even without having to wait for military deployments, she was going to have some explanation to do about her tardiness.

The monthly reports she sent in to update on her assignments and progress allowed her to continue without having to return, so it was somewhat strange to be headed for the system now. Her last report had indicated that she would be there in a matter of days, days which had expired more than a week previous. She fully expected to be berated for her tardiness during her check-in but she hoped that the medical records submitted with her report would alleviate some of the punitive response.

Gliding away from Lovus, she observed with no small amount of interest as the three bands of wide white and grey rings slowly circled in their orbit around the massive planet. Most of the ringed planets she knew of were uninhabitable, enormous gassy and frozen places where almost no life could exist. Even the few rocky ringed planets she had learned about were not inhabited, which left this as the only inhabited planet that had its own rings to her knowledge. She wondered what it would be like to see the arcs of frozen ice and rocks on the horizon each morning and whether it caused strange weather or seasonal patterns. Atmospheric control devices were often used to make sections of otherwise uninhabitable planets safe for survival, often used for outposts and other long-term settlements, so perhaps something similar was used to control Lovan weather. If enough of them had been used, they could completely terraform an entire planet, allowing comfortably habitable zones even on an otherwise unsuitable ringed planet.

She dismissed the thoughts as they flickered through as nothing more than idle curiosity, as she had no real, lasting interest in uncovering those answers. Her natural curiosity was already engaged in further, more personal, matters.

Red flashing lights on her console changed to blue, alerting her once she was far enough outside the Lovan system to safely activate the compression drive. Since it had already been programmed to automatically activate, she felt the familiar tug at the same time she registered the flashing lights. The first handful of times she had used the spatial compression drive had been disconcerting, leaving her somewhat nauseated as a result of the unnatural motion. Years of use had acclimated her to it, so now she barely even noticed when it turned on. Less than half an hour later, she was within direct communication range of her home system.

"M'Tarl Nox," she called over the comm, "reporting in."

"We read you, Nox," a voice responded. "Status?"

The voice on the other end of the comm was unidentifiable as to whether the speaker was male or female but it hardly mattered. Regardless of who was on the other end of the comm, the information requested and delivered was always the same. "The ship was successfully placed onto the planet known as Earth," she explained.

"Was it located?"

"Affirmative. The targets located and retrieved the ship approximately one week after it was placed. I have confirmed that they have returned to their primary system."

"Understood and well done. What about the secondary target?"

"Negative. I was unable to gather the intended information from the secondary target." She paused for a moment before adding, "there were complications."

"What kind of complications?"

"I was captured by the secondary target. That capture resulted in medical treatment and the delay in my report."

"Understood. Please submit all reports on both targets."

"Understood." The process was standard, similar to what happened every time she checked in, with the exception of her reporting her own capture. Because she knew what to expect, all of her reports had already been compiled and ready to submit, including the surprisingly large medical file she had received from the hospital. With a short series of commands in her console, she sent the reports along their way. A yellow transmitting light switched to green, indicating that the message had been successfully delivered and had remained secure in transport.

Her physical presence was almost never required when she submitted her reports to the Voivode Council so, rather than heading toward the planet, she stayed in outer orbit, matching her own flight path to that of a nearby space station. Briefly, she considered docking to it in order to get a fresh meal and some new supplies she was running low on, but ultimately decided against it. If the council did decide her presence was needed, she didn't want to have to make them wait while she undocked and set a new course, nor did she want to cut her meal short. She did, however, place an order to the station so that once she had her new assignment from the council, she could pick up everything she needed on the way out.

She didn't have long to wait for a response. Just as she finished submitting her order to the station, her comm unit flashed, indicating an incoming message. "Nox here," she responded.

"Nox, the council would like you to confirm the loss of your psionics, as reported on page seventeen of your report."

"Confirmed. I do not currently have use of any of my psionic abilities."

"Understood. Stand by."

This was a change in protocol and M'Tarl paused, her hand hovering over the console, as she wondered what it meant. "Probably being pulled off active duty," she mused. "At least until I regain my psionics." Or until she could prove she could be effective without them. There were plenty of agents for the Voivode Council who didn't have her particular abilities. They were hardly a requisite for employment with the group, after all. In her case, they had simply been an added bonus.

"M'Tarl Nox," a different voice spoke up. Unlike the previous voice, she recognized this one as belonging to Shuja Caolan, the leader of the Voivode Council and her eyes widened as she wondered what that meant. Why would a man such as that be in direct communication with a relatively low-level field operative such as herself? "With your psionics gone, this council no longer believes that you will be able to continue your mission."

That lined up perfectly with what she had already assumed. The mission to which she had been assigned had been given to her due to her psionic abilities, without them the chances of her succeeding were slim, particularly considering that she had already been captured once. She was disappointed, certainly, but not surprised. It still didn't answer the question of why Shuja Caolan was the one communicating this information to her.

"Further," the message continued, "without your abilities, you are to be retired from your position, effective immediately."

The light on her console went dead, indicating that the connection had been severed. There was no room to question what she had just been told. While she had already expected to be relieved of duty for a while, she had never considered that she would be fired outright. M'Tarl blinked in surprise at the black, silent comm panel, trying to comprehend what had just happened. "What the hell?"

Rather than spending her time focused on what had transpired, she refocused her mind onto what she needed to do next. Without the guidance of the council, she was completely free to do as she saw fit. "Whatever that will be," she grumbled to herself.

She wasn't worried about income. She had spent frugally the whole time she had been employed by the Voivode Council and most of her regular expenses had been reimbursed, so she had a decent amount of savings to last her. The main thing that she would miss was ready access to the resources of the council but that could also be easily rectified. During her years, she had developed plenty of resources of her own.

Her first order of business was to update the order she had just placed. If she was no longer being reimbursed for her expenses, she didn't need everything she had requested.

Additionally, a couple of the items were restricted, so she doubted that they would be dispensed anyway. Once the updated order was submitted, she docked at the station to await delivery and get the fresh meal she had foregone earlier. "I guess my next question," she mused to herself as she ate, "is what do I want to do now?"

The possibilities, unfortunately, were as endless as the galactic night.

# IRON GAUNTLET

Shuja Caolan had bigger and more pressing things on his mind than just the loss of one of his operatives, effective as M'Tarl Nox had been. She had been up for promotion, a trajectory that had been cut as short as her career with the Voivode Council now was. As soon as he ended the communication with his former operative, he turned to one of his companions. "We have received confirmation that the ship was successfully delivered to the Queen of Diamonds and the Knave of Spades. Have we heard anything further from the Deck?"

Until ten years previously, the organization known as the Deck had been nothing more troublesome than a band of thieves and miscreants, satisfied with stealing a few supply ships and other valuable goods at somewhat regular intervals. Since that time, the group had undergone a substantial change in their hierarchy, which had made them a much larger threat than they had previously been. Although the Deck, as a group, had never been what one would consider lawful, they had at least been quiet. When the man known as the King of Clubs had assumed control, however, that had all changed. They had become a truly dangerous force, using overt power grabs and assassinations in order to achieve their ends, whatever those ends may be. Much as the Voivode Council had tried to uncover their motives, both before and after the power shift, no information had been forthcoming.

With the reported death of the original

leadership, the Voivode Council had believed that there was no way to return the group to its former ways. Shuja had never been completely convinced of their demise, a faith that had driven him to send operatives in search of the missing leaders.

"We believe that the Queen of Diamonds and the Knave of Spades have already begun to make contact with some of their former allies." Calen Merott was the liaison between the Voivode Council and the Interplanetary Government, little more than a bureaucrat who was often sent to meet with the council when they needed to either acquire or dispense information. This particular visit had been arranged to dispense. Everything from his carefully maintained hair to his dark brown suit to his shiny wingtip shoes screamed office worker, his ever-present briefcase a perfect accessory to the position. He never opened the briefcase on his visits, so its contents remained unknown.

"What kind of reports do we have on this?"

"When they disappeared and the King of Clubs took over, we placed monitors on many of the communication channels that we had already uncovered. Most of those went silent after the takeover and had remained so for the last five years or so. The last one dropped approximately four years and seven months ago."

"Are you saying that we don't have any means of tracking what they're up to?" Shuja still had no idea how M'Tarl Nox had managed to track down the elusive pair and, now more than ever, he could have used her unique abilities. Tracking the pair would apparently be more difficult than he had expected. Had they really recovered the pair only to immediately lose track of them again? The idea was almost unthinkable.

"Not entirely. While those communication channels have been silent, we maintained our tracking on them. A short while ago, almost all of them began receiving incoming calls. Most were never received or had only short communication after pickup, but a few were longer in length. We believe these to have all originated with Diamond and Spade."

"I see." That had been their hope in sending the ship to the planet on which the pair had been stranded. In response to the increasing threat by the new, more violent, version of the Deck, the Voivode Council had voted less than a year previously that they would do everything within their power to support the Queen of Diamonds in retaking her position as the leader of the Deck. This decision had been largely supported, if not outright suggested, by the Interplanetary Government. It was their combined hope that by restoring the former leader to power, the violence caused by her group would diminish, reducing the threat level to everyone they encountered. "If they do manage to resurface," he mused, "that would bring an end to a lot of our common problems, would it not?"

"We suspect so. Most of our information indicates that if she returns to a position of power, she will have the ability to stop the Deck's reign of terror and bring them back to the peaceful group they previously were."

"Good, then. It sounds like things are well

under way, in that case." With a dismissive nod, he turned back to his console.

"There is more."

"Hmm? What's that?" Shuja looked up to see the man still standing just where he had been. Apparently the meeting was not concluded after all.

"We have recently uncovered information that a portion of the Deck have already begun to splinter away from the core group."

"Is this because of the communication attempts by Diamond?"

"No. This began over a year ago, before the ship was delivered, while everyone still believed her to be dead."

That didn't sound well to Shuja's ears. "Tell me more about this splinter group."

"They call themselves the Iron Gauntlet. From what the Interplanetary Government has gathered so far, the current hierarchy of the Deck is already anticipating some sort of problem within the Deck, as they started shuffling resources to the Iron Gauntlet sect almost immediately after its formation."

"Why am I only hearing about this now?" Shuja demanded. "I should have been informed of this a year ago." If the most violent portion of the Deck was merely reforming into a new group, that partially defeated all of the efforts he and the rest of the council had put into Diamond's recovery. Had he known this was a factor, he would have reconsidered at least some of his planning.

"I understand your position, but our information is as current as it could be. You were not informed before now because, simply, we didn't know until now. This information was only recently uncovered and it was just as much of a surprise to us as it is to you."

Shuja seethed. He had just recently received reports that one of the planetary systems under the Voivode Council's watch had been attacked. At first, he had believed that it was an attack resulting of the ongoing strife between Triad and A.T. Now, given this latest information, he suspected there may have been much more at play. "Does this have anything to do with the attacks within Voivode space?" He glanced over at the comm, wondering whether or not he should rescind his last order, but decided against it for the time being. He was particularly uninterested in sending a rescinding order while Merott was still present, as it had been by his directive that his agent had been released in the first place. Even with her powers gone, Nox had still been a highly skilled asset, one he already wished was still under his command.

"It may. Our concern is that the Iron Gauntlet intends to expand their holdings even further."

Shuja didn't like the sound of this one bit. It was bad enough having to deal with the onslaught of A.T. using their forces to control populations through fear and assassinations. It was out of concern that the Deck may one day join forces with the larger and more dangerous might of A.T. that he and the rest of the council had agreed to the Interplanetary Government's suggestion of resurrecting the Queen of Diamonds in the first place. Now, it appeared, not only did they have to deal with one murderous army of thugs but that a second was quickly gaining power. Just how much worse were things going to get?

"We believe that they may continue expanding into the Onoquoi system."

Calen's words hit their mark, as the Onoquoi system was the home system of the Qadar and the Voivode Council. Any attack, real or perceived, upon their home was automatically given the highest of priorities. Too many times now, the Qadar had witnessed as entire solar systems fell beneath the unyielding onslaught of A.T. The last thing that Shuja, or any other member of the council, wanted was to see such an occurrence within their own system. The stakes were simply too high to sit back and do nothing. This was about as bad as the news could possibly get.

A.T., whose name was practically untranslatable from its original language, had been a part of the galactic landscape almost as long as Onoquoi itself had been. From what Shuja understood, it had once been a planet-based civilization, similar to how other races had begun, but when they ran out of resources on their own planet, they began to expand into other neighboring planets as well. They cleared their own solar system of valuable materials and substances within a decade, swarming from planet to planet like an acidic cloud. They probably would have stayed within their own bounds for a lot longer than they did, had it not been for the fact that their solar system only had a scant handful of planets for them to strip mine.

They grew in strength as they expanded their operation, landing in massive numbers on inhabited planets and enslaving the local populations, forcing planetary residents to assist in the gathering of valuable resources. Seeing how they operated, many of the other space-faring nations in the galaxy, the Voivode Council included, had watched their activities with interest, keeping a close eye on the group in case they moved too close to their own borders. By the time anyone realized how truly dangerous A.T. had become, it was almost too late to do anything about it.

Triad, the least expected of these groups, had been the ones to take a stand against them. They had watched the same activities as the rest of the galactic population, but rather than waiting for the worst to happen, they had prepared. Over two decades, as A.T. gathered their might, Triad had grown in strength as well. Finally, when Triad was ready, they mounted a counterattack.

That counterattack had been devastating to both sides of the fight. Losses had counted in the tens of thousands, injuries far more. But after almost seven years of fighting, Triad drove A.T. back to their home system and set up a blockade to keep them in place.

A.T., for their part, hadn't been excited about being locked in place and had mounted a counterattack of their own. They pushed back against the Triad forces, gaining ground as they did. Over the years since then, the pair had been locked in battle, sometimes hot and sometimes cold, each side trying to hold their line or gain just that little bit of ground. Triad's aim had been to safeguard the neighboring solar systems from the A.T. invasion, at least long enough for others to help the residents evacuate, which the Voivode Council had assisted with.

Other groups had joined the fight as well, very few of whom had been effective. Triad continued to be the only true stopping force keeping A.T. from the galactic dominance they so clearly desired.

"We do not like the idea of having military movements so close to our borders," Shuja admitted. "We are not fans of war and we want no part of this battle."

"From the way things sound from my position," Calen said, "you may not have much of a choice in the matter. They are coming, regardless of you and your people's views on war."

"I shall contact Triad immediately."

Before Shuja could even reach for the comm, Calen interrupted him. "You cannot."

"What do you mean I cannot?" He looked up at the standing man, enraged. "We are members of good standing within the Interplanetary Government and we deserve to be protected just as much as every other planet under your watch. That is, after all, what Triad exists for."

"You and I both know full well that protocols must be followed. We in the Interplanetary Government already know of this threat and we are taking steps to deal with the situation. If such a time as it becomes necessary, we will notify Triad and send them to assist you and your people."

"This is outrageous." Shuja shot to his feet and faced the visitor. "You cannot expect us to sit back and watch as our people are attacked."

"Of course not," Calen looked down at the Qadar, who stood almost a foot shorter than him. "You can defend yourselves as best you see fit while we continue our evaluation." He picked up his briefcase from the table, turned, and headed for the door. "Once a decision is made, I will contact you."

Shuja continued seething until long after the annoying liaison left. He and the rest of the council had fully supported bringing Triad under the Interplanetary Government's control, a move that he believed would suit both Triad's financial needs as well as his own people's needs for continued military assistance. Assurances had been granted at every step of the way that, should the need ever arise, Triad would be ready and willing to come to their assistance. Commander Moore had personally assured him that so long as there was a single troop member available, he would always send reinforcements.

The red tape that needed to be shoveled through in order to request such assistance had been unforeseen. Before Triad had moved beneath the Interplanetary Government's umbrella, assistance had been only a comm request away. Merott had made it clear that such interactions were no longer allowed, causing a pit of discomfort to begin growing deep in Shuja's belly.

# GOSSIP

Without a clear direction in what she needed to do next, M'Tarl finished resupplying her ship and sat at her console, weighing her options. She was close to Onoquoi, a place she hadn't been to in many years. Although it would be interesting to see her home world after so long, she had no real draw to go down onto the planet's surface. Despite having originated there, the cloud-covered sphere beneath her ship felt less like a home to her than the openness of space did. She had no friends, no relatives, nobody to visit or anyone who had missed her in her absence. More of her life had been spent off-planet than on, a fact that didn't escape her as she viewed the glistening globe.

Well, technically, she had relatives. But they didn't know that.

Most people would be bothered by the knowledge that they, as far as their entire world was considered, didn't exist. M'Tarl was not one of those people. She had chosen this life deliberately, with much consideration of what that would mean for her and her future. For the life that she had chosen, having people to miss her was a liability instead of the blessing they were for other people. Personal attach-ments, be they great or small, could only bring danger. Not just to her but to others who got too close as well. Her life was already fraught with danger enough without having to bring new levels into play. The absolute last thing she needed was to invite more problems, more danger, more difficulties into her life.

The loss of her powers, on the other hand, bothered her greatly. While aboard her ship, she was safe, as the ship itself was optimized to perform many of the same functions as her abilities had done. The most advanced sensors and optics on the open market continuously scanned the surrounding area, notifying her of every potential threat, big or small. Internal sensors within the ship's body constantly monitored everything from air quality to atmospheric pressure and gravity, ensuring that she would be notified the moment anything crept toward harmful or even inconvenient levels. While many of the sensors had been paid for by the Voivode Council, none were based in technology she no longer was allowed to have. Nothing could get within range without her knowledge and plenty of reaction time for her to decide what to do about it.

Well, that assessment wasn't entirely correct, she recognized. Her sensor range wasn't nearly as expansive as her psionics had been.

Plus, there were things she had been able to pick up that the sensors were simply incapable. Out in space, it wasn't as noticeable that she couldn't hear the thoughts of others since there was nobody nearby to hear. In a crowded canteen such as the one she had just been in on the station, however, it was blaringly obvious. The most reasonable solution was to stay in space, as far away from other people and their hidden thoughts and motivations as possible. While that solution sounded reasonable, she already knew it was anything but.

What she needed was information.

Her path decided, she set the controls to exit the system. Regardless of which star system she was near, information was currency, a currency in which she was much poorer than she was comfortable. If she couldn't simply pick up the information directly from the minds of those she encountered along her travels, filling her vaults with the necessary currency to know everything she needed, she would have to do the next best thing.

She had to return to Lovus.

After a lifetime ensuring that she maintained a level of distance between herself and any place to which she had recently traveled, it seemed strange and unnatural to return to Lovus so quickly. After all, she had only been there a few days previously. However, she had only been on planet long enough to get the medical treatment she had required and hadn't stayed any longer than medically necessary, such had been her hurry to submit her reports and get new orders. If anywhere in the galaxy was safe for a return visit, Lovus should be that place. Now she needed to return for two reasons: first, she had been asked to return for a checkup, a checkup she hadn't initially intended to follow through with but now it appeared she had no better alternatives. With just a little luck, the doctors may have uncovered a solution to her most pressing issue. M'Tarl had very little faith in that prospect but the hope settled into the back of her mind regardless.

The second reason was her true purpose in

returning to the ringed planet. She needed to have a word with the Gossip.

Getting back into Lovan space was marginally easier than it had been the previous time, not that her last trip had been difficult at all. This time she had a statement from the doctors requesting the return visit, a handy excuse for why she had returned so quickly. As such, she was guided down to land in the same parking lot that she had been directed to the last time she had been there. Different from the last time, however, no doctors came out to greet her. This time was not considered an emergency.

She debated on getting her checkup first but quickly decided against it. The sun was already over the horizon, bathing the landscape in dazzling light, so she knew the Gossip had already begun to gather. They were an early morning bunch, after all.

From the outside, the nondescript little diner didn't seem to be a very important gathering place. It was moderately sized, larger than the corner deli but smaller than the expansive restaurants closer to downtown. Brown and orange shades offered protection from the rising sun, casting shadows through the windows to the diners inside. Pale wooden doors with stained glass windows and brass handles admitted entry to a carpeted dining area where a long bar stretched from one end of the room to the other, comfortable seating for those enjoying a solitary breakfast. The scent of fresh coffee and hearty bacon flowed through the air, tickling the senses.

A handful of patrons enjoyed their breakfasts inside the building and away from the sun but the majority were outside on the sunny patio, sipping at coffees and teas or other assorted beverages and nibbling at fruits and muffins. Despite the humble appearance, the back patio of this diner was the gathering place of one of the most information-laden groups known throughout the galaxy. The Gossip met at the same time on the same day of every week to chitchat and discuss all manner of current events. When the weather turned cold, they remained on the patio, warmed by a series of large space heaters provided by their hosts. Since it was late spring, there was no need for the added warmth from the heaters, as the sun provided ample heat for the group.

Some members were nothing more than curious locals, gathered in order to glean bits of information from the assortment of conversations and to add their own to the mix, but others were directly or indirectly involved in some of the most powerful governing bodies across the galaxy, including Triad. They never discussed secret matters openly but, if one was to listen closely and pay attention to the clues, and if one knew what to look for, one could glean information not available anywhere else.

M'Tarl stepped carefully through the gathered Qadar on the patio and found an empty chair at one of the small round tables. She didn't know any of the others seated with her but it hardly mattered. As soon as she sat, she was immediately included into the conversation as though she had been there from the beginning.

"The station took a direct hit and was completely destroyed. Nothing left but rubble, from what I heard. From a ground-based mecha, can you believe it?"

"I bet they're hoping the war doesn't end, just so we can keep them on our side and not have to let them go back home."

"Pshaw. There's no way we'd keep a war going unnecessarily just to keep a handful of mecha pilots around."

"Maybe we wouldn't, but you know it's been suggested."

"Besides, even if they did end the war, where would they go? Their home world is in ruins."

"True. Now that A.T. has had their run of the place, there's not much for them to go home to. I heard it's barely even inhabitable anymore. I suppose there's still an atmosphere there, though."

"Yes, there is an atmosphere, but the air quality is poor and most of the ground water has been contaminated." The speaker clucked her tongue disapprovingly. "If they do ever decide to go back there, they're going to be sorely disappointed."

"Indeed. They'll definitely need someone to help clean up that mess. Nobody could do that on their own."

"Speaking of mecha, the Tournament's coming up soon. I heard they were planning to enter this year."

"Wouldn't that be exciting? I would love to see them in action, not just in reports."

"As would I, but you know as well as I do that active Triad members are barred from entering the Tournament. It's an unfair advantage."

M'Tarl poured herself a cup of tea and pulled a handful of juicy red grapes out of the bowl of fruit in the center of the table. While the current topic was interesting, she didn't see how any of it could be useful to her. The Gossip was highly inclusive, as any who wanted could join without the need of a formal invitation, but it was also highly exclusive, as only those of the Qadar race were truly accepted into the group. Outsiders, those from other backgrounds, were not banned outright but they rarely bothered to join the group. Keeping up with the rapid-fire pace of the conversations that flowed through the Gossip was deliberately difficult and most who attended a gathering out of idle curiosity soon decided that the residual head-aches weren't worth what little information they had been able to gather or share. It was far easier to manage a meeting with one or two members of the Gossip away from the group if information sharing was needed.

She turned her attention to a different por-tion of the conversation when she overheard something familiar.

"The Deck is being a bigger problem, too."

"I had heard that someone finally heard from the Queen of Diamonds."

"Really? That is big news indeed. She's been gone for so long!"

"I wonder where she's been."

"Maybe she got ousted by the group and she's been hiding deliberately."

"That wouldn't happen. Her people love her."

"Indeed, that is true. Additionally, there is

no way she would tolerate what has become of her Deck during her absence."

"She was on a planet called Earth," M'Tarl interjected. "Far outside of communication range."

"Well that explains why none have heard from her. How did she escape?"

"She found an abandoned Vergling ship, as I understand it."

"This Earth that she was on, is it near Vergling space?"

"I thought the Verglings had plenty of communication satellites in their quadrant. How could she have been outside of communication range?"

"It wasn't actually that close to Vergling territory," M'Tarl explained. "There was just a ship there that she found and took control of."

"My, isn't she the resourceful one."

"If what you say is true and she really has returned, that should minimize the damage the Deck is doing."

"That is our hope as well. She has always been against violence of any kind, so there is no way she would allow this behavior to continue."

"She has to be appalled at what's been happening in her absence."

"As I understand it, there is a different group that has already begun forming from some of the Deck. The Iron Gauntlet, I believe they're called."

"Aren't those the more dangerous of the bunch? I wonder what they're up to now."

"Nothing good, you can bet. They've set up outside the Tyrannus system and have been terrorizing everyone there for months now."

Nothing M'Tarl had added to the conversation had been deemed classified and news of the Queen of Diamond's return had already begun to spread, so there was no harm in giving them additional information. There was no way to know what, if anything, the gathered Qadar would do with the information, but it didn't matter. All of the information would become readily available soon enough. Knowledge that the Iron Gauntlet was forming and where may be useful later, so she filed that away in case it was necessary.

"I heard something recently," she changed the topic when the conversation lulled, "about a psionist who lost their powers."

"Oh my, where did this happen?"

"I don't have all of the details but there was some sort of a violent interrogation involved."

"Was it A.T.? Or perhaps this new Iron Gauntlet?"

M'Tarl shrugged. "I just know there is someone out there looking for a way to restore their power because of this."

"I had heard of that. They were treated right here at Midway General."

"Oh, good. If anyone could restore their powers, they can."

"Not quite. The doctors haven't been able to reverse it yet."

"Has this ever happened before?" This had been the real question M'Tarl had been leading the conversation toward, so she took the opportunity as soon as it arose. "I don't think I've ever heard of a case like this."

"I don't think so." The rest of the group agreed, dashing M'Tarl's hopes for a quick resolution. "At least, not without substantial brain damage involved."

"We can do some investigation into this," one of them offered. "As soon as we know anything, we will be certain to make our information known to that poor psionist." The speaker was one of the oldest Qadar at the meeting, a female named Galeah. M'Tarl recognized her on sight, as did most Qadar who saw her. Galeah's husband was second in command of Triad, so if anyone had the power and resources to find the information M'Tarl needed, this was her best chance. It was Galeah's presence that had caused M'Tarl to choose her current seat and while she was disappointed that the elder Qadar didn't already have the information she needed, she trusted in her promise.

Satisfied that she had accomplished what she had come for, even if the information hadn't been what she'd wanted to hear, M'Tarl turned her attention to more of the surrounding conversation, interjecting bits and pieces where she had information and opinions to share. She stayed until she had consumed multiple cups of tea and had eaten approximately a third of her own body weight in the never-ending bowl of fruit before excusing herself.

From the diner, she headed back to Midway General. She had little hope that the doctors had some up with a solution for her, particularly after the information she had gathered from the Gossip.

Just as she had expected, Dr. Aditi did scans of everything that he had been unable to do previously, all of which came back with negative results. He and his fellow doctors looked at everything they could and determined that she was healthy, despite the absence of her abilities.

"You haven't said anything about brain damage," she asked, remembering the information discussed in the Gossip. "Is that something I need to be worried about?"

"I'm not seeing any damage points. Had there been anything to see, I would have told you about it but as far as I can tell, everything looks healthy." He clicked on his computer for a moment and turned a monitor to show her the brain scan results.

"We are still seeing activity in your brain," he explained as he showed her the test results. "Specifically in the area that controls your abilities, same as we were seeing before. We can see that you are still trying to activate them, either consciously or otherwise, so we remain hopeful that the pathways will open on their own in time."

She wasn't surprised. Most of her abilities were latent, meaning that she didn't have to focus at all to turn them on and off, much as how most people didn't need to pay attention to their lungs in order to continue circulating oxygen to their systems. It was likely those abilities and her own subconscious efforts to use them that were causing the spikes. Briefly, she wondered what the spikes would look like while she tried to use one of her intentionally-used abilities but decided the time spent on taking more scans would likely be wasted, as there wouldn't be much more than a satisfaction to her curiosity as a result. "So what should I do now?"

"Like I said, we're still optimistic that your powers will return at some point. For now, I will continue researching on my end to see if I can come up with anything new to try but it's looking like you will just need to be patient."

Nonplussed but unsurprised, she accepted the doctor's prognosis. "Anything else I need to know?"

"We would like you to come back for another follow-up in another few months, or sooner if you see any indication that your abilities are returning."

# CHAPTER 6

# POSSEVILLE

---

Feeling completely defeated despite all of her best efforts, M'Tarl decided it was time for a pick-me-up. Although she didn't have family and friends on her own world, that didn't mean she lacked friends on other worlds. Her travels and assignments had taken her far and wide, crisscrossing the galaxy multiple times over in her years of service, so she had made contacts on almost every inhabited planet she had spent any length of time on. Most of her friends had fallen more under the category of minor acquaintances and necessary contacts but a small handful of them were ones she felt truly comfortable among.

She waved down a transport and headed for a small island off the highway, halfway between Midway and the mainland. Although the island didn't have an official name, it was colloquially known as Posse Island due to its most famous – or infamous, depending on which version of the myriad legends one heard – inhabitants. The Triad special forces unit known as Posse owned the entire island, only half of which was open to the public. Stretches of inviting sandy beaches covered the perimeter of the island, dotted by tall palms gently swaying in the salty ocean breeze with plenty of sun umbrellas, beach towels, and insulated coolers indicating the area's attractiveness as a recreation area. At the end of the beach, nearest the roadway and parking area, an island-themed tiki market sold refreshments, diving gear, sun umbrellas, beach towels, and all manner of supplies that could be needed by the beachgoers. The other half of the island was restricted access, hidden behind a deceptively strong stone and concrete wall and designated only for use by Posse and those they allowed within their home.

Posseville was exactly what M'Tarl would expect to see if a group of pre-teen adolescents were allowed free reign to makeover a luxury resort. The entrance was unmistakable, as the area could only be accessed via an immense steel-gated archway with the name of the estate emblazoned across it in two-foot-tall, scripted letters that were illuminated in colorful neon at night. The grounds beyond the gates were sculpted and tidy, with clean grassy areas and pockets of brightly colored flowers. The drive itself was smooth pavement lined with shrubbery that had been shaped into fantastical figures, including seven- and eight-foot-tall representations of the residents themselves. As she approached the house, she could see the backyard waterslide, a glistening affair in the shape of an erupting volcano, the slide itself fashioned to look like flowing lava, rising over the top of the seven-story mansion. It was the only waterslide M'Tarl had ever seen, in all of the worlds she had traveled to, that came with its own elevator.

The members of Posse were nothing if not hedonistic.

It was in the backyard that she found DJ, lounging at the edge of the pool at the base of the slide. Posse as a group consisted of five members known as Mouse, Troll, DJ, Gazer, and Elfe. As M'Tarl understood it, others were occasionally stationed with Posse, sent to live and work with them for training and other reasons. If any of those groups were there, none were visible.

"Hey, stranger," he looked up at her from under the wide-brimmed straw hat he wore. The hat barely fit over the waist-length dreadlocks that grew from his head, each of which was decorated with colorful beads and other assorted jewelry. More rings adorned each of his toes and fingers, causing him to make a clicking sound with every step he took. Other than the hat, he was bare from the waist up, deeply tanned skin soaking up as much sun as he could manage. His lower half was covered only by a pair of knee-length board shorts in a red camouflage pattern, the least inconspicuous color for such M'Tarl had ever seen.

"Hey yourself," she responded as she dropped into one of the deck chairs, sighing with pleasure as she sank into the thick cushions. "How was the last mission?"

"Not too shabby. Kinda boring, actually." He propped himself up on an elbow, jewel-laden hair flashing in the light as he moved and faced her more fully. "How about yours?"

"Not great. But I survived, which is the important part."

"That's true enough. You look terrible."

"You look great yourself, thanks. But this?" she chuckled, "This is after being to see the doctors. Twice."

"No kidding? What happened?"

"You know I can't tell you that."

Despite the tacky design of their villa and the apparent youth of their members, M'Tarl wasn't deceived. Each member of Posse was at least her own age, likely far older. They, as did many other long-standing members of Triad, all kept their youth due to regular applications of age regression therapies. She wasn't sure whether it was due to vanity or to keep their edge as a special forces unit but no member of Posse ever appeared to reach the age of thirty human years.

As they talked, a tall, buxom blonde in an impossibly small forest green bikini and heeled white sandals came out to join them. She broke into a wide smile when she saw the visitor. "Hey, M'Tarl, I was just talking about you."

"Yeah? Anything exciting?"

"Possibly." She settled into a chair on the other side of DJ. "I just got off the comm with Galeah. She had some interesting things to say." As she settled back, she kicked the sandals off, letting them fall to the side of her chair.

M'Tarl had a feeling she knew what was coming, a feeling that had nothing to do with her nonexistent abilities. She had known that Galeah wouldn't waste much time investigating the psionic damage she had described in the Gossip and she had further suspected that Gazer would be one of the first people Galeah would contact. After her own husband, of course. "How's she doing?"

"She's doing well, keeping herself active. I'm sure you're already aware of that."

M'Tarl nodded. "She always has been the active one."

"Anyway, she mentioned that one of the members of her Gossip stopped by today, asking about missing psionic abilities." Her smile faded as she spoke. Some may have been fooled by Gazer's admittedly effective bimbo persona, but those people would quickly discover their mistake as her appearance was both deliberate and manufactured, a disguise she frequently used to encourage others to view her as harmless. There was no way to fool Gazer, as she was one of the most powerful psionists known to the galaxy. Gazer's abilities were second only to Mouse, leader of Posse, who was easily the strongest of all of them. "I may have a way to help."

"You have my attention."

"You need to understand, first of all, that this is merely an option, not a recommendation. I am in no way advocating that you follow through with anything I am about to say at all." She sat up and turned to face M'Tarl, crossing her legs in front of her on the lounge chair as she spoke.

M'Tarl's brows raised in surprise. Part of the lore surrounding Posse was their complete and total disregard for rules and regulations, not to mention consequences to their actions, unless they had been deployed. For Gazer to express any amount of caution, she must be very concerned indeed. "Understood. I will take your information as nothing more than that. Anything I do with that information is at my own discretion."

Gazer stretched and wiggled her perfectly pedicured pink toenails. "I have a... well, I wouldn't exactly call him a friend, but I don't know of a better term to use. His name is Jeoh.

He might, and I really mean *might*, be able to help you come up with a solution."

M'Tarl's brow refused to budge. She had heard of a person named Jeoh, just as most who traveled the galaxy had at least heard of him. Legends could be found everywhere of the mysterious traveler who appeared without warning, helping or harming those who he encountered with equal measure. Some believed Jeoh to be a survivor of early A.T. experimentation, searching for a way to undo what had been done to him. Others believed him to be an agent for the Interplanetary Government, sent from place to place on the most secretive of missions. Still others suggested he might work for a different faction entirely, or perhaps was the secret leader thereof, a faction who was biding their time and waiting for the optimal opportunity to strike at whatever their target – or targets – may be.

Still more people, M'Tarl included, believed the stories to be nothing more than bored wives' tales to awe and frighten the gullible. If he existed at all, he was likely not much more than a normal person of whatever race he happened to be. For Gazer to mention him as someone she personally knew was an absolute shock. "I've heard the name," she finally said.

Gazer nodded. "I figured you would have. Like I said, he might be able to help you uncover the cause of your... problem. He can be difficult to reach, though."

"From what I have heard of him, I believe it. He's reported to be even more reclusive, even more of a nomad, than even I am believed to be."

Gazer laughed. "That's true enough, I suppose." Her expression sobered. "But you should be aware, he will likely want some sort of a favor in return."

He wouldn't be the first that M'Tarl had needed to trade favor for favor with. She accepted both the warning and the small piece of paper Gazer handed over. "This is his contact information. If you use it," she kept a firm grasp as M'Tarl tried to take the page, "tread carefully. While he will follow any agreement you make with him to the letter, he will exploit any loophole he may find."

# CIRCUMVENTING THE RULES

---

Lazy clouds floated by, visible through the wall of windows next to Ryan Moore's desk, but he paid them no attention. "You know," he said finally, "the news has been running a lot of stories about us lately." He turned his attention to Coffee, his personal assistant, who sat across the desk from him.

"The news is always running stories about

us." Coffee didn't bother looking up to respond. "We're newsworthy, so there's always something they want to share with the public."

"True, but these stories indicate that we are preparing to go to the Cardiss system." Ryan sighed and pinched the bridge of his nose between his fingers. "Another interesting part of this is that the Queen of Diamonds herself called me to request that we stand down while she regains control over her people."

"Yes, I recall that started quite the chaos here when she did." Triad's trace of that call had ultimately revealed that it had originated in Ryan's own office, resulting in an overhaul of their security. Unsurprisingly, they had found nothing suspicious within their own communication system but that hadn't stopped the Triad security team from continuing in their efforts, trying to track down the source. "I had been under the impression that we hadn't received orders to go there yet."

"We haven't. But that hasn't stopped the news from saying we are." He took a drink of his coffee and settled back again. "Apparently even the Queen of Diamonds herself is following us on the news. I probably should have suspected something like that but it's still a bit of a surprise to hear from her so directly. Much as I would like to, we can't do much of anything about the Deck, even had she not called. Given the agreement between us and the Interplanetary Government, our hands are pretty firmly tied until they send us orders." He steepled his fingers on the desk again. "Well, technically we could do something, but not until they attack us first. So far, that hasn't happened, and I don't have any reason to believe it will."

"Diamond could request your assistance too, couldn't she? If things go badly for her and she is unable to retake the Deck, that is."

Ryan shook his head again. "There is no official alliance between us and the Deck, or with her specifically. Since they're not part of the Interplanetary Government, and none of them are Triad conscripts, there's absolutely nothing we can do to help them." It galled him that he now had to wait for official authorization from people who moved slower than the average garden slug instead of being able to mobilize immediately to help those in need. No orders to move on the Deck, regardless of how much damage they had been doing, had ever come. He'd half expected to discover orders against the Queen of Diamonds herself, now that she had made her presence known, but none had come. Not that he wanted to see such orders, as he respected the enigmatic woman quite a bit.

Probably, he realized, more than he should.

"Do any of those," he motioned to the stack of paperwork on the edge of his desk, documents he hadn't had the opportunity to read through yet, "have anything to do with the group known as the Iron Gauntlet?"

"Iron Gauntlet? I don't believe so." Coffee shuffled through the papers quickly, much more familiar with their contents than his boss at that moment. "Nope, doesn't look like it. I don't think we're familiar with that group. Should we be?"

"I've only just heard about them recently

myself," Ryan explained. "As I understand it, the Iron Gauntlet is forming from members of the Deck, some sort of a splinter group of the most dangerous and violent members, apparently in anticipation of their absentee leader's return." He took another drink of his coffee before continuing, "and now, we've also received no official word from anyone on the Iron Gauntlet. Am I going crazy, or is that just a little suspicious?"

Coffee didn't have to check before responding. "It does seem odd. Should I put in a request for information?"

Ryan finally tore his gaze away from the view beyond his window and looked at his assistant directly. "Not from the Interplanetary Government. I'm losing more and more faith by the day in their willingness to share information with us." He chuckled mirthlessly. "So much for their promise of full disclosure. I suppose we should have known better. But we do still have plenty of contacts of our own, so let's send out some feelers to our allies, see if they've come across anything interesting lately."

"If the Interplanetary Government does send orders to move on the Deck," Coffee said as he stood to leave, "what will our response be?"

Ryan blinked at him for a long moment. He had been pondering just such an occurrence himself. Of all the potential targets in the galaxy, the Deck was one he was least excited to send troops after. Not because he believed there would be much difficulty on his peoples' part but because he just plain didn't want to attack them. Not if the Queen was actually regaining control. If her efforts went badly, he may be willing to rethink his position but he had faith in the enigmatic woman. "I really don't know," he admitted finally. "Now that she has returned, the Deck should also return to its original peaceful, if larcenous, ways. I can only hope that no such orders will be forthcoming.

"The Iron Gauntlet, on the other hand, is a different matter entirely. Between you, me, and the clouds outside, had we been given the authority to attack when the threat had first been uncovered, the problem would have ended before it even began." His brows lowered and his mouth hardened in irritation. Now, he suspected that any orders he received, if he received any at all, would be too late. While he had plenty of units he could send out to stop the latest threat, the longer they were required to wait, the more firmly entrenched the group would become, making Triad's efforts that much harder.

The last thing he needed was another drawn-out war.

"All of the information I have on the Iron Gauntlet indicates that they are based in or near the Tyrannus system"

Coffee winced at that bit of news, recognizing the name. The planets in the Tyrannus system were not members of the Interplanetary Government, so they were unlikely to request Triad assistance with this or any other problem. "Do we have any trade agreements with them? Anything at all?"

Ryan shook his head. "Nothing. No treaty, no trade agreements, nothing whatsoever." Without some sort of alliance in place, the Interplanetary Government had no reason to send Triad in to assist. Tyrannus would fall, overtaken by the Iron Gauntlet, unless the Tyrannians did something themselves to stop it.

Much as he hated it, it was the truth. Ryan had personally seen, time and time again, how planets and entire solar systems had come under attack by one invading force or another but, due to the lack of trade and treaty agreements with the Interplanetary Government, orders had demanded that Triad maintain a distance from the action and Ryan had been forced to watch helplessly as planet after planet was overthrown due to lack of action on the part of him and his troops.

In all his years as commander, that had been the hardest thing to stomach, one that continued to give him indigestion. Losing a battle was something he could understand, as no military in the history of the galaxy had ever gone undefeated. Every battle entered into was one that could be lost, and he had accepted that fact many years before. Not even entering the battle zone, particularly when his troops could easily turn loss into victory, was a completely different matter.

Recently, he had begun searching for a way of circumventing such problems and had acted upon such only once since joining the Interplanetary Government. When a planet he had been monitoring had been attacked by A.T. forces, he had sent troops after them regardless of the lack of trade agreements. Triad and A.T. had been at war for long enough for Ryan to justify at least an initial deployment to the planet's surface. It had been those troops who had made contact with the planetary residents after driving away the first wave of attackers and who had invited members of the planet to join Triad in their fight to defend their world. Many members of the planet, at least those who were left alive after the first wave of A. T. soldiers, were eager to join, giving Ryan the perfect opportunity to sidestep the rules and regulations in order to help those who needed him.

After all, protecting those who couldn't help themselves was what Triad had been founded for and what he was determined to remain standing for.

"Oh, there's one other piece of news you might be interested in." Coffee shuffled through the reports and moved one from the middle of the stack to the top. "The latest cognitive implant designs are done and ready for testing. They just need your approval to move forward."

"Fantastic. I'll take a look at those first."

Cognitive implants, better known to the general public as brain jacks, were intercranial devices that allowed the wearer to connect mind to machine with an array of the most highly advanced technologies used throughout Triad. They allowed people to pilot machines with lightning-fast commands, almost as fast as the thoughts that drove the communication itself. The response time when using a brain jack was almost high enough so that the machine moved reflexively as the pilot became more and more a part of the vehicles they drove. This would be the fourth version of the implant, the most advanced version so far. From what he had been told so far, not only was the response time much faster than any previous model, this one was even capable of self-repairs, minimizing the need for regular maintenance. When it was complete and ready for implantation, it should just give them the edge they needed to finally make some headway in their front-line battles.

At least, he hoped it would.

Moreover, since this was now the fourth generation of devices, that meant that he could release the first generation of brain jacks to the general public, a request that most had been clamoring for years to get their hands, or at least their skulls, on. By his estimation, sales of the brain jack would do wonders to close the financial gap so that he and his people would be less dependent on credits from the Interplanetary Government.

The sooner that happened, in Ryan's opinion, the better for all of them.

# JEOH

---

M'Tarl considered the piece of paper she had been given once she was on her ship and waiting for takeoff clearance. She watched the icy rings circle past, steady and unhurried in their orbit, wondering at the caution Gazer had recommended, caution that was well outside the woman's normal behavioral pattern. "Why are you so worried about this guy?" she wondered. "Particularly if you consider him to be something resembling a friend." Of all people, she never would have expected Gazer - or any member of Posse to be more accurate - to show such hesitation over a single person. "I mean sure, there's rumors about this guy, but they can't all be real, can they?" She wondered whether Gazer's apprehension was due to personal knowledge about the reported stories about Jeoh or whether there were other reasons, reasons M'Tarl didn't yet know about.

Deciding that heeding the woman's suggestion despite the apprehension would be the best means of moving forward, she debated on where she should set the meeting. This was hardly the first clandestine meeting she had set up, so she had a wide assortment of places that were perfect for such occurrences. With the little amount of knowledge she had on Jeoh, his reputation notwithstanding, she decided that the home advantage would suit her the best. She set a course for a station orbiting Signus IV, one of her favorite out-of-the-way stations that had everything she could possibly need.

The station wasn't the biggest she had been to, nor was it the smallest. It wasn't one of the primary stations used for any military activities, other than serving as a resupply waypoint for some of the long-transport ships. It was quiet and had a decent diner and bar, which was what she was after. They had food shipments delivered often enough that the meals served at the restaurant actually tasted good, a vast improvement over the travel packets most places carried. One thing that was quickly discovered by anyone who spent long stretches of time in the emptiness of space was the value of fresh food when it was available.

When she arrived, however, she discovered that her favorite nice, quiet station was anything but quiet. Military-grade ships filled over half of the docking stations, forcing her to wait longer in line for an opening than she had expected. As she slowly circled the station, waiting for her turn to dock, she wondered at the quantity of ships there. All of them had Triad insignia coating their hulls, announcing to any who dared come too close how dangerous of a decision that could be. When she finally gained access, she ended up at the very end of the central column in a spot barely large enough for even her small ship, squeezed between a pair of massive battle cruisers. On the station, people in Triad uniforms swarmed the area, far more than she had seen packed into one place in a long time.

At least, outside of normal Triad-controlled areas.

Perhaps this wasn't an optimal place for a meeting after all, she thought. Conversely, perhaps this was the best place to have a meeting with Jeoh. If he truly was as dangerous as Gazer had made it sound, having so many active military personnel on the station could only help to keep him sedate. Her decision made; she found a reasonably quiet corner of the communication deck. There were small, enclosed spaces designed for privacy, each of which had an assortment of comm panels to reach every area of the galaxy, whether by direct contact or relayed through communication satellites. Since she had no way of knowing where she was calling, she activated the relay comm panel, entered the contact information and opened the line.

On the other end of the line, the comm was picked up almost immediately, before a full set of tones had finished sounding. "Hello?" A deep masculine voice answered in a thick accent that she couldn't place.

"My name is M'Tarl Nox," she introduced herself. "I was given this contact information by Gazer, and I am looking for Jeoh. Is he available?"

"This is Jeoh."

From his flat response, she assumed he wasn't interested in small talk, so she got directly to the point. "I am looking for a way to restore psionics to someone who had their abilities taken away. Gazer said you may have some knowledge in this field. Is this something you can help with?"

"Hmm..." he responded. "Perhaps. I will need more information." His manner of speaking was slow and drawn-out, unusual from M'Tarl's perspective. Perhaps it had something to do with his native language, whatever that may have been.

Strange accent aside, she had expected such a response. "I don't have a lot more information at this time," she explained, "other than telling you that the person in question is registered as a class two psionist who underwent a rather, shall we say violent, series of interrogations. Once that was done, the abilities were no longer functional. Brain scans all show that there is no brain damage, the area is still viable and active, and all scans appear to show that the psionic abilities aren't blocked, they just can't seem to manifest. The person in question was seen by Triad's physicians multiple times but even their doctors don't know how to restore it."

"I've heard of something similar to this before," he admitted. "Psionic abilities can be a tricky thing and most brains are complicated; the smallest of things can cause problems. Usually they sort themselves out, returning on their own in just a few days. Perhaps it would be best to just wait."

"That was the doctor's suggestion as well, but it has been quite some time now with no improvement and this is a bit of an urgent matter."

"I will do what I can to assist you with this," he decided after another lengthy pause. "Assuming, of course, that you are able to meet my requirements."

This is what she had been waiting for, what Gazer had warned her about. "What kind of requirements are you referring to? I have money, if that's what you're looking for." She watched from the corner of her eye as uniformed troops jogged down the corridor behind her, wondering again what so many of them were doing there.

"I don't need your money. But as for my requirements, perhaps it would be best discussed in person."

"I can do that. Where would you like to meet?"

"I'm not allowed on Lovus, or anywhere within the Lovan system. For that reason, I will request that you meet me somewhere neutral for both of us."

M'Tarl blinked in confusion. "I'm not on Lovus currently," she said. "Nor am I anywhere within the Lovan system."

"Your call contains a code that indicates you are on a secure Triad line. If you are not on Lovus or within that system, I can only assume you are in a different Triad-controlled area."

"I am on a station outside of Signus IV." She looked around, noticing again the amount of Triad personnel on the station. Had they over-ridden the entire station's comm system to run with their security?

"Ah, that would explain it. That station recently had an incident which required the deployment of Triad personnel. I had assumed the security codes meant that you were on their planet."

"Does that mean you can come here to meet with me, or do we need to meet elsewhere?"

"That station will suffice. I will be there in twenty-seven hours and thirty minutes."

That was a remarkably specific arrival time. "There are a lot of ships here," she explained, "so waiting for a dock to open could take some time."

"I'm not worried about getting access to a dock. I simply need enough time to finish a project I am working on and to prepare for the journey. I shall see you in twenty-seven hours and twenty-nine minutes." The line closed, ending the call as abruptly as every portion of the conversation had been.

She spent the remainder of the evening resting on her ship, wondering what kind of incident had caused Triad's response and how Jeoh had known about it before knowledge was available to the general public. Was the incident he mentioned something to do with him? While she knew that she would be perfectly safe on the station, there were too many people and she didn't want to be constantly surrounded. Moreover, it was unnerving to have so many people around and not be able to hear the constant buzz of their thoughts. The silence was truly deafening. She reached up, almost without thinking, to feel the reassuring form of the ring suspended from her neck. Just the simple act of touching it soothed her, as it always had.

Her wounds had continued to heal, some of them were nothing more than faint remnants of what they had once been. Even the largest ones, wounds she had originally been certain would leave lasting disfigurements, had healed nicely. While they would still leave scarring as a testament to what she had undergone to receive them, they weren't nearly as noticeable as she had initially worried they would be. The doctors at Midway General truly were every bit as talented as they were reputed to be.

As with most Qadar, she didn't need many hours of sleep to be rested, which gave her plenty of time to reflect on her situation. Just before her scheduled meeting time, she headed for the agreed-upon canteen to await Jeoh's arrival. While there were a handful of Triad people in the canteen, waking up and breakfasting in order to prepare for their own day, the area was less than half filled. The time frame he had given her had been quite specific. So specific, in fact, that she wondered whether or not he would actually arrive at the precise minute he had indicated or whether he was simply trying to appear mysterious. Many people she had dealt with previously had adopted strange mannerisms that were nothing more than a means of keeping the people around them off-guard. Tactics such as those rarely caused her any trouble, at best she viewed them as amusing oddities and at worst obnoxious irritations. Regardless of which Jeoh's turned out to be, she would be ready at the designated time.

She knew the moment he entered the room. Even had she not been facing the only entrance she would have known. Many of the Triad personnel shot to their feet, hands on their weapons and ready to draw, turning to face the man as he entered. Even those who didn't respond to the perceived threat so overtly moved slightly to keep an eye on him as he walked across the tile-covered floor of the canteen. Her glance moved surreptitiously to the closest timepiece, a clock on the wall next to her, which indicated he had arrived at the precise moment he had stated the previous day.

Jeoh was well over seven feet tall and impossibly thin. Dark hair, streaked with white, fell across his shoulders, the striped pattern continuing into the small, well-groomed beard on his chin. His clothing hung from his body like a series of capes, slowly waving as he walked, making it appear as though he had far more joints than most humanoids possessed. His height had initially indicated that he was a Tet, but he was far too thin to be of that race and only had the biological equipment for binocular vision. Ignoring the attending military presence and their reaction to him, he walked calmly to M'Tarl's table and took a seat across from her, his legs appearing to compress rather than fold beneath him as he sat.

"My requirements are simple," he explained without preamble. "First, and this is not negotiable, I need a genetic sample from you personally."

"A genetic sample?" Of all the things he could have asked from her, that was probably the least likely thing she had expected him to say. "What do you need that for?"

"It is for my own research and will not be shared with anyone. You have no need to worry that it will be used against you in any way."

She considered his request, knowing she had little choice. Although his answer seemed sufficient, it was nowhere close, as he hadn't actually answered her at all. There was no indication of what type of research he intended to do with the sample. If the man was going to help her, she would have to agree. Luckily for her, the sample he had requested would not violate any of her confidentiality agreements, as there was nothing confidential about her, genetically speaking. "Other than that?"

"I will need officially notarized permission to visit whatever system you are in at any time."

His requests had somehow become even more bizarre. "Why do you need such a thing?"

Slowly, the people at neighboring tables returned to their meals, apparently no longer interested in the newcomer. Except, of course, the Triad personnel. Those people only pretended to return to their meals, keeping a wary eye on Jeoh.

"That is not my requirement, it is a condition applied upon me. I cannot travel to anywhere, outside of a small section of allowed space, without both explicit permission and expressed purpose. For both your sake and mine, the permission needs to be granted before any further actions can be undertaken."

Remembering that he hadn't been allowed in Lovan space, she wondered how extensive his restrictions were and what, precisely, he had done to bring such down upon himself. She knew that he was feared across the galaxy, although most seemed uncertain of why they should be so afraid. Discussions about the skeletal man were often held no louder than a whisper. Despite all of the stories and legends about him, he didn't appear to be much of a threat. If he was truly as dangerous as rumors made him to be, he would have been locked away long before. For him to be a free man, or some semblance of free, there had to be more to the story that she hadn't yet uncovered. "I can do those," she agreed. "So you'll help me, then?"

Some of the Triad soldiers moved to get a better angle on the conversing pair. Used to working in a more clandestine manner, M'Tarl wasn't comfortable with the increased attention on her, despite knowing that most of the attention was on her strange companion. She caught a glimpse from the corner of her eye as one of the men whispered into his comm unit, calling for reinforcements, she suspected.

"Collect for me ten genetic samples," he said, "each from different systems and none that are on this list." He held out an infopage, which she reluctantly accepted.

The infopage contained an extensive list of items found on multiple planets, pages upon pages of nothing but itemized list. As she scrolled, one of her eyebrows lifted. "You've collected all of these?"

"Samples of them, yes."

"And all you want is ten that aren't on this list?" Scrolling to the bottom of the list would take a while and reviewing all of the listed planets and items would take even longer. Hopefully this portion of his requirements wouldn't be too difficult to meet, as there were planets to which M'Tarl had traveled that weren't on any usual trade or communication routes.

"Correct."

The doors of the canteen opened and the dull murmur of conversation among the military force that surrounded her grew slightly as more reinforcements joined the guards. Again, M'Tarl wondered at the response. This couldn't all be because of them, could it? Just what was so dangerous about this man?

"There is one other thing," he smiled, an expression that appeared uncomfortable on his face and did nothing to make M'Tarl feel calmed or reassured. If anything, it had the opposite effect. "I would like a download of your memories, just in case you have encountered something that will be useful to my research."

"Absolutely not." The other requests he had made, although unusual, weren't personally reprehensible to her. Her memories, on the other hand, were to be hers and hers alone. "If that is one of your requirements, I believe this conversation is over." She stood to leave. As optimistic as she had been that the strange man may have been able to help her regain her psionics, there were some lines she was unwilling to cross, prices that were too high to pay. Even the loss of her psionic abilities, should that loss turn out to be permanent, was not enough of a tradeoff for her to agree to such a condition.

"Wait, please." His face returned to its normal state of ambivalence. "It is not an absolute requirement; I had merely hoped you would agree. I have an alternative, of course." He steepled his fingers on top of the table before folding them together and tapping his thumbs against each other.

Still not sure she could trust him, knowing that if he had the means to access and download her memories there wasn't anything she could do to stop him, she looked back toward him. "What's the alternative?" She didn't bother to conceal the doubt in her voice.

"One favor, to be paid at an undetermined point in the future."

If there was one thing M'Tarl hated, it was open-ended favor requests such as the one he made. However, she didn't see much by way of alternatives. She was in a bind and not only did he already know it, he appeared more than willing to capitalize on it. Additionally, she had been expecting such a request. Gazer herself had warned her that he would likely ask for it. As much as she disliked such arrangements, it was far better than the alternative. "If I agree," she turned back to face him fully, continuing to scroll through the list, "you will leave my memories alone?"

"Correct. Once I have the genetic sample from you, the notarized permission, and these ten samples, I will be at your disposal until this matter is resolved and your memories will remain yours and yours alone." He smiled again, just as uncomfortably as the last time. "I give you my word."

His words echoed her own thoughts closely enough that she narrowed her eyes, wondering if he had been scanning her despite her refusal but his face gave nothing away. There had been no telltale pressure that would usually indicate mental scans, but that meant little. Powerful enough psionists could access the entire set of memories belonging to their target with little to no physical indication of the intrusion. Without knowing what kind of abilities Jeoh had, she had no way of knowing whether he was powerful enough to perform such a feat. Finally, she relented. "Fine. I agree to your terms."

Even as she spoke, his arm shot out toward her, a minuscule needle in hand. He had taken a small amount of her blood before she had fully registered the movement. "Let me know when the rest is ready," he said as he unfolded from the chair and rose to his feet, "and I will come to meet you, wherever you may be."

Once he was out of the room, the military

personnel began to settle once more, all of those who had been paying surreptitious attention to his actions finally returning to their breakfasts in earnest. M'Tarl did the same, reaching up to feel the necklace that was hidden beneath her shirt. She wasn't sure what the genetic sample he had taken from her would reveal but hopefully it wouldn't cause her even more problems in the future.

What in the galaxy had she gotten herself into now? And how much would she end up regretting this decision?

# BLOODHOUND VIRUS

The Gossip was a wonderful place to catch up with old friends, find out the latest in current events, and to share a meal and a cup of tea with people not seen often. One never knew who would make an appearance on any given day, so Galeah made it a point to be at all of them.

That wasn't always the case as, before she had retired, she had been away from home more often than not. During that period, she had relied on more structured means of getting the information she desired but that information had always been centered on military activities such as troop movements, things uncovered on target planets, new technological developments, and even estimated death counts from both sides of the conflict. She had loved the job, feeling personally that the advisor position had been perfect for both her interests and her ability to sort through massive amounts of information and glean the truth from within. The decision to retire had been a difficult one, as she felt a sense of purpose within the ranks of Triad that she hadn't felt elsewhere for a long period of time. However, the job had become stifling and constraining, particularly now that Triad was conscripted beneath the Interplanetary Government. They had their own advisors who sorted through the information, so what she got was a heavily watered-down version of what she already understood to be the truth.

Even after having retired from that position,

she continued to preserve good relations with most of the people she once worked with in an official capacity. Unlike most who retired from such a coveted position, she had maintained her security clearance, which allowed her access to much more restricted information than most people knew about. Some within Triad had been concerned about her continued involvement in the Gossip, assuming that she would begin sharing secret, restricted information but that had never been the case. While Galeah dispensed information and wisdom at every gathering she went to, it was always information based on what she had learned outside of official channels and never anything that could be considered confidential. More importantly, she had been able to return to Triad to share information she had gathered from the Gossip. In some cases, she had given the military information that they hadn't previously uncovered on their own. Because of that, not only was her continued presence within the Gossip tolerated, it was encouraged.

All of that being understood and accepted, there was still information that even her relationship with the Qadar community and sent via official channels to Triad weren't enough to fully understand. "Details", as she was known to say, "are the key to comprehension." Without all the details, the knowledge could never be complete. Finding herself in such a situation once more, she tapped her foot restlessly in the elevator of the Triad Towers, eager to head for yet another source of information.

Her car, a speedy pale green roadster with a little too much chrome to be considered tasteful and a specially-modified engine that could propel the vehicle much faster than most considered safe, a car that really should have been restricted to competitive racing, waited where she had parked it in the same designated spot she had used since her first day reporting to Commander Moore. Although there had been brief discussion about it after her retirement, mostly from those who wanted to assume ownership of her coveted spot, she had maintained her control over it in no small part due to her continued presence in the offices of the buildings that soared high overhead. Now, as the engine roared to life, she pressed the button to lower the roof, allowing fresh air to circulate through the car while she tucked and folded her massive skirts, arranging them so that she could sit comfortably without the reams of fabric blowing around in the wind. Whenever the weather allowed, she preferred to drive in the open air. She idled out of the parking area, stopping for a moment to chat with the parking attendant before slipping her sun shades over her eyes and pulling out onto the street in the direction of the highway that led off Midway Island and onto the mainland.

Partway to the mainland, she took a small, unobtrusive offramp that exited the highway and decreased her speed considerably as she dropped down onto the small island below. Rather than turning to head toward the recreation area, by far the most popular destination for those on the road upon which she drove, she headed for the secure end of the island, passing beneath the neon archway and along the topiary-lined drive. She chuckled as she spotted the latest topiary designs, as only Posse would find it appropriate to have larger-than-life caricatures of themselves along their front drive.

"Gazer, my dear?" she called as she opened the front door and stepped into the cavernous building. "Are you about?"

"Upstairs," a voice called down from higher in the building. "I'm in my office."

She lifted her skirts and headed for the stairs, her slippers hardly making a sound on the marble tile underfoot as she moved. She climbed easily to the third floor and headed down the carpeted hall, walking past ceiling-high windows that let in both plenty of light and a breathtaking view of the ocean. The top half of each window was formed of stained glass, which bathed the hall in a rainbow of colors. Those windows had been Galeah's own suggestion when Posse had first begun design-ing their home and she was pleased each time she walked past that they had accepted her idea. At the end of the hall, one deceptively nondescript door was ajar, which she pushed further open in order to enter the room.

This room was a truly enormous space, although from the doorway it hardly appeared to be such. Over half of the area was walled off with glassteel doors, each of which revealed banks of computer equipment beyond. No windows opened to the outdoors but lights in every color of the rainbow, similar to those in the hallway, glowed through each of the clear-paned doors, some steady and bright, others flashing in a steady pattern. Unlike the light in the hallway, however, these lights had nothing to do with the sun outside, as they were all indicators on one set of machinery or another. Although Galeah had no idea what most of the equipment did, she knew that they were all important pieces of Gazer's network.

And expensive. She had personally seen the invoices for much of the equipment and had been shocked at the costs involved. She had approved expenditures for warships that had cost less than this bank of computers.

The rest of the room was dominated by

a U-shaped mahogany desk that had seven monitors placed above it. Some of the monitors had figures running across the screen, some had camera views of places Galeah didn't recognize, and a couple were dark. Behind the desk, leaned back in a leather chair with her sneakers comfortably propped up on a corner of the desk and a bowl of tortilla chips on her denim-clad lap, Gazer scanned the bank of information, occasionally reaching out to press a button on her keyboard. Today her blond hair was pulled back in a loose ponytail, the ends hanging freely down her back.

"That's a nice gown," Gazer looked over and smiled at her visitor. "New?"

"Yes, I just received this one a week ago."

"I like the color, it's a nice shade of burgundy. But then, I'm a bit biased on that."

"I particularly like the embroidery, it's exquisite."

"So what brings you by today, other than to show off the new addition to your wardrobe?"

"The call we had a while ago, wherein I

described the loss of one's psionic abilities. I would like to discuss this matter further."

Gazer nodded and dropped her feet to the floor with a muffled thump, setting the bowl of chips on the desk as she leaned forward. "Had a feeling you'd be wanting to talk about that at some point. What is it you're wanting to know?"

"I would like to know more about this person who lost their abilities," Galeah explained. "I didn't have much by way of information to begin with and you know how secretive the hospital can be about divulging patient records."

"Oh, I know. Particularly when that patient isn't a resident of Lovus. The person they treated is officially registered as an Onoquoi citizen."

"Are they, now? I hadn't realized." Galeah pursed her lips. "That would indicate that the person in question is a fellow Qadar."

Gazer nodded. She didn't have to be explained the camaraderie Galeah felt for all who shared her heritage. "It's a bit more than that. The person isn't just any old resident of Onoquoi. Until recently, they worked directly for the Voivode Council."

"Until recently? Were the two events related?"

"I believe so. I can't imagine that the Voivode Council would have much use for a psionist without any abilities." One of the monitors next to her beeped quietly. Without looking, she reached over and entered a series of keys, silencing the sound.

"Have you met with this person? Or have you just been tracking them?"

"I have met with her. Actually, she's an old friend of ours. A few years ago, she helped us out on one of our observation missions and we've maintained a pretty decent relationship with her since then. In fact, she stopped by just after you called me."

"In that case," Galeah settled herself onto one of the guest chairs and arranged her skirts comfortably, crossing her slippers at the ankle, "please tell me all that you know of this person."

"Is this an official inquiry or are you just curious?"

"Mostly my own curiosity but you never know what people will one day ask about."

Gazer chuckled. "That's true enough. Okay, I'll tell you what I know about her." She explained about what she knew of M'Tarl's history with the Voivode Council, which she had researched years before, shortly after their initial meeting. She further explained about how M'Tarl had been on the receiving end of a rather brutal interrogation, pulling up a medical report on one of her screens to show the extent of the damage. "The doctor overseeing her care is one I am familiar with; I've had to see him for some minor issues of my own. They healed her up as best they could, physically, at least, but there wasn't a whole lot they could do about her psionics. Since all of the scans they took are showing activity in that area of the brain, they're assuming her abilities will return on their own."

"You don't seem so sure."

Gazer sighed and shook her head. "Nope,

and if someone came up with a way to short-circuit someone's psionic abilities, I want to know more about that. Not just the who and how of it happening in the first place, but I want to know how to fix it in case it happens to one of us." She leveled her gaze on her visitor. "I'm sure we both understand how dangerous that would be to some of our own people."

Galeah nodded sagely as she perused the screen, clucking her tongue sympathetically as she saw description of injury after injury. "Is this what you've been focused on? Are you working on a means of restoring such an occurrence?"

Gazer's face twisted to the side. "Indirectly. There isn't a whole lot I can do myself, but I'm not exactly a specialist in these kinds of things." While Gazer had plenty of fingers in the biomedical field, this was definitely outside her purview. She looked at her friend for a long moment before explaining, "I sent her to meet up with Jeoh."

Galeah sucked in a deep breath. "I know I don't need to tell you how dangerous that may be." While she may have been on friendly terms with the man as well, she also understood precisely how manipulative and cunning he could be.

"I know. And I warned her to be really careful with him. She understands the risks involved in meeting with him as well as the importance of careful wording in any contracts, verbal or otherwise, she agrees to."

"Do you really think this is the best idea?"

Gazer shrugged. "He's easily the most experienced with pretty much anything relating to psionic abilities, particularly how they relate to the physiology of the host. He's done more in-depth studies of brain chemistry and mapping every neural pathway than even we have, probably more than even A.T. has. If anyone can come up with a way to restore her abilities, he's the one to do it."

Galeah's face continued to register her uncertainty, so she added, "You should also know that I went to meet with Jeoh personally before they met up. I made sure that he understood what his limitations in this would be, as well as what the repercussions would be if he decided to cross any lines."

"I still don't like it," Galeah said as she traced one of the embroidered patterns on her skirt, "but I understand the logic in such a decision. If you believe this will be her best chance for successfully recovering her abilities, I trust your judgment." She adjusted her skirts and rearranged her seat for a moment before changing the topic. "There is another matter I would like to discuss with you."

"What's that?"

"I heard mention of a weapon that was used recently, one that seems strangely familiar to the Bloodhound virus."

Gazer sucked in a deep breath, her eyes darkening at the words. "I don't want to talk about that." An almost tangible barrier dropped down around her, an instantaneous and automatic defense her psionic abilities made as a response to what they felt was a mental attack. Had it been anyone else bringing it up, the very mention of the Bloodhound virus would have elicited a much stronger reaction.

The Bloodhound virus was the biggest black mark on Gazer's record, one that she was loathe to discuss openly. Years previously, shortly after her recruitment into Triad, Gazer had developed a virus that could bypass all known security at that time. That in and of itself wasn't so bad, but the fact that it could also be used to unlock and open all computerized doors and hatches was the real nightmare. There had been concerns about its use, fears that it could grant unauthorized access to secure Triad areas, but it had never been used for such a breach.

What it had actually been used for was much, much worse.

During the second half of the first A.T. war, after all attempts at treaties and ceasefires had been either refused outright or accepted and then ignored, the advancing enemy force had completely overwhelmed the Triad military. Their technological advancements since the beginning of the war had proven to be far more substantial than Triad had been led to believe, which left them at a disastrous disadvantage. Star system after star system had been overrun with Triad's forces consistently and methodically pushed back, unable to stop their momentum or take back even a single planet, let alone any of the overthrown systems. Conversations within Triad became desperate, as many began feeling that they had no way to possibly win the battles they were faced with, feelings they voiced openly. General consensus was that Triad had lost the war and all that was left was to offer surrender and lose gracefully. Commander Moore had been weighing such an option, but everyone agreed that if Triad surrendered to A.T., there would be nothing left of Triad or Lovus, let alone any of the other planets who relied on Triad for their own safety.

Left with what she felt was no better option to decrease the damage and gain ground against their unstoppable enemy, Gazer had taken it upon herself to unleash the Bloodhound virus on every enemy space station she could get a lock onto, which had been many.

Tens of thousands had died instantly. As the

airlock doors opened into the void of space, everything was sucked out into the vacuum. Between the lack of air and the freezing temperatures, there was no hope of survival.

Most of those casualties had been military.

Hundreds of civilians had been killed.

Shocked and guilt-ridden by the loss of life that she alone had been responsible for, Gazer had immediately submitted her resignation, waiting for charges to be brought up against her. Although she had initially pled guilty, the charges against her had been reduced to the most minor form and all records of the trial had been sealed, information about the means she had used deemed too vital to Triad security for the general population to know about. Responsible for the end of countless lives, possibly entire family lines, many of whom hadn't been combatants, she had received nothing more than a slap on the wrist and her resignation had been refused.

That blackout of all information about the virus had caused rumors and other forms of false information to spread like wildfire, both about the virus itself and its source.

"I know," Galeah said gently, "and nobody is saying that it has been used again. This was just similar enough that people have wondered whether you may have some ideas on how it was done and whether we need to adjust our defenses in case a similar attack is directed at us." Familiar with Gazer's resistance to the topic, she wasn't afraid of the powerful psionist's defenses. It had been understood for almost longer than either of them could recall that she would never use her abilities to harm those she cared about.

Gazer still appeared reluctant, but she didn't outright refuse so she pressed the issue. "The Queen of Diamonds used this weapon against the King of Clubs when she took control of the Deck away from him. It caused a complete shutdown of all the base's systems when it was used."

Gazer let out a breath and her shoulders relaxed slightly, her eyes returning to their normal color and the protective wall dissipating.

"I heard about that and had a similar thought. It definitely hasn't got anything to do with the Bloodhound virus. I don't even think this was a virus-based attack at all. As far as I can tell, it was based off an EMP weapon."

Electromagnetic Pulse weapons had also been widely used during the early days of the war but almost everyone had shielding in place to prevent the use of such weaponry. For one to prove so devastating now was astounding. "How was an EMP weapon effective against the shielding?"

"I'm not sure yet. Ryan contacted me as soon as he heard about the attack, wanting to know if we're at risk from them too." As with many of the highest members of Triad, Gazer didn't bother using the commander's formal title in general conversation. She had known him since he was young, since they were both young, and there was simply no need.

"Are we?"

"Yes." Her answer was both simple and devastating. "This one completely bypassed all of the base's EMP shielding, so we've been working on coming up with a way to increase our shields against it." She indicated one of the monitors, which appeared to be running some sort of testing schematics. "So far, we don't have a lot but we're working on it and pretty sure we'll have a solution fairly shortly." Her brows furled. "So long as it's not used against us in the meantime, we should be fine."

"We?"

Gazer nodded. "Tripp and Mike are helping me on this too. When I told them about it, they were highly concerned."

Tripp and Mike were familiar names to Galeah. Co-owners of World Industries, they had a vested interest in safeguarding their equipment against EMP and similar types of attacks. The vast majority of Triad equipment came from World Industries, particularly all of the new, most technologically superior machines and vehicles known to the galaxy, so this impacted millions upon millions of credits in potential lost revenue. If Gazer was this concerned about the attack, Tripp and Mike had to be exponentially more so.

"As far as we can tell, Diamond is the only one who has this type of device, so we're assuming that it's her own design," Gazer explained. "Well, hers or Knave's, as its rather hard to tell which of them is responsible for it. If you talk with Ryan before I do, I'd recommend staying on her good side, at least until we have protections against this. I'm going to recommend the same when I turn in my next report."

"Well, then, I will let you get back to your investigation. I can see that you have many important things to work on and I don't want to take up too much more of your valuable time." Galeah stood to leave. "Thank you again for both your hospitality and your information. As always, both are greatly appreciated."

"I'll stop by and visit for longer once I have this resolved," Gazer promised. "I feel like I'm close to a breakthrough, so I don't want to go too far from my computers." She smiled at her friend. "I'll even bring the tea."

"Understood." She smiled in return. "I look forward to your visit."

# TASKMASTER

Remembering Gazer's warning about trusting Jeoh, M'Tarl thought carefully about how to create the notarized permission form he had requested. Normally, such forms were minor affairs, mere formalities where the absolute wording within them could be subjected to interpretation with some freedom but in this case, that would not suffice. Gazer's warning about his exploitation of loopholes ensured that the writ needed to be as iron-clad as possible. The very fact that he required such official permission caused her additional concern. "Why does he even need this in the first place?" she asked her empty cockpit. "Sure, he's been banned from a couple areas but that doesn't mean that he's been banned everywhere, has he?"

She ran a search of him, trying to see how widespread his restrictions were, but no results appeared. Confused and somewhat concerned at the lack of findings, she furrowed her brow and thought. "Are his restrictions more extensive than I thought?" If that was the case, she needed to be much more careful when coming up with appropriate wording for his permissions, just in case she could somehow end up liable for wrongdoing on his part. The last thing she needed was to cause additional trouble for herself, as she had enough problems of her own to deal with.

"The bearer of this writ," she read what she had come up with for the third time, "is hereby granted permission to accompany M'Tarl Nox for a time period of no greater than one year from the date this document is signed." That seemed pretty clear and concise, with little room for interpretation. "Will one year be enough?" she wondered. "Or is it too long? Hopefully it doesn't take him that long to fix this." Deciding it was acceptable, she moved on to the next. If she needed to give him an extension, she'd deal with it then.

"The bearer must stay within a one-mile range of M'Tarl Nox at all times while accompanying her and must obey all local laws for any planet or system of planets into which they travel." That should keep her from being held liable for any laws he may break. She wasn't certain about the radius as it sat, as a mile could be both a very small and a very great distance, often simultaneously. "Is that too far?" she wondered. "Do I need to shorten it?" Alternatively, anything less than one mile seemed to be too close to keep him reigned in. Should she need some form of privacy, she didn't want him to be constantly underfoot.

Finally, she decided a mile would just have to suffice.

"If at any time the bearer breaks any local laws, the bearer will be subject to immediate eviction from the system in which the offense was made. If the law enforcement or governmental agencies request the bearer to leave the system at any time, regardless of reason or lack thereof, the bearer must leave the system immediately and without argument."

She re-read the entire document a fourth, then a fifth time, making minor adjustments to the wording to ensure there was no interpretation available, no loophole to exploit. Finally satisfied, or as close to satisfied as she knew she would become, she set the document aside. It would be notarized the next time she was planet-bound.

Next on her list of requirements to gather, she examined yet again the list on the infopage he had left with her. "Ten genetic samples from at least ten individuals," she mused. "Each of whom are from a system not already on this list." The list was extensive, covering most of the areas to which she had already been. "Each sample from a different planet," she muttered as she made notations on her own list, crossing off planets as she came across them on his list. "That doesn't leave very many to choose from." As she perused further, she realized that there were plenty of planets she had visited at one point or another, planets that were not indicated on his list.

There were other planets and other systems as well, ones she hadn't already been to but that she had knowledge about. "Not exactly thrilled with the idea of handing over a bunch of genetic samples," she admitted again, "particularly since I still don't know what he plans to do with them." She wondered whether the people she took the samples from would give them willingly or whether she would need to use subterfuge to obtain them. That line of thought inevitably led her to consider the sample he had taken directly from her. She had no way of knowing whether he had already started his research, whatever it may be, on that sample or whether he was waiting for her to complete the rest of the gathering before he started. "Regardless," she said finally, "I need to get moving. No progress will come of sitting here and not doing anything."

As she set a course in the autopilot for the closest system on her short list, she stopped. Her hand hovered over the controls for a moment as realization sunk in. "I was making this a lot more difficult than it needed to be," she said. While it had been clear that Jeoh's intentions had been for her to collect genetic material from sentient creatures on each of the systems she went to, he hadn't stated so much explicitly. "He just said genetic samples. There was nothing about what kind of source they came from." She grinned to herself, recalling Gazer's words about Jeoh's tendency to exploit loopholes. "You're not the only one in the business of exploitation."

She finished setting the autopilot and turned back to her list as the computerized system performed its function, a low vibration announcing that the drives were warming up. She considered how many plants, insects, and all manner of genetic materials she could gather from the systems she had identified. "Much easier than getting them from humanoids, that's for certain." She didn't even need to limit her search to planets inhabited by sentient beings, she just needed to find planets with life of any variety at all. Sentient life was rare, but microbial life was almost everywhere, there were even some kinds that didn't require a planet to live on, capable of surviving even in the frozen void of space. This was going to be a lot simpler than had initially appeared.

As she traveled from planet to planet, collecting samples to fulfill her end of the agreement, she kept a close eye on her abilities. Rather, on her lack thereof. The doctors at Midway General had assured her that they were confident her abilities would return on their own. If that happened, or when it happened, if she was being optimistic, the core need for her to work with Jeoh would become moot. If she didn't need him to restore her powers, then there was no need to continue working with him. Disappointment met her every time she

attempted to use them, each attempt resulting in the same dismal failure she had experienced every time since crawling from the hole
in the ground.

Getting the samples, now that she had a plan
on how to do so, was easy enough. The only
part that was time consuming was the period
of travel between planets. Since she couldn't
use the spatial compression drive while she
was in a system, inhabited or otherwise, the
vast majority of her travels were spent either
entering or leaving a solar system. Those were
the periods where she was most calm, most at
peace with her current situation. Out in the
open air, even on an abandoned planet, she
felt exposed. That sensation was much worse
any time she was on an inhabited planet, not
knowing who was near her, paying attention
to her, plotting against her. "This must be what
it's like for people who don't have psionic abilities," she recognized. "How do they function
like this?"

Furthermore, she found the expanse of
space to be comforting, as she had from the

first time she had left the surface of her home planet. Whenever she was feeling anxious or nervous, on edge for any reason at all, all she needed to do was to sit and stare into the familiar darkness of space and her worries would ease, melting away completely before too long. Even while still within the confines of a solar system, she was still more comfortable between planets than on them. Knowing that she wasn't stuck was a great help to her mind-set, realizing that no matter what happened and who she did or did not work for, there were countless places to go, to explore, to learn everything she could about anything she wanted. While she was in the vast emptiness of space, there was nobody at all with whom she needed to concern herself. All she needed, all she had ever needed, was the freedom to travel as she saw fit. Now, she had that freedom in greater quantity than she had experienced at any point of her life before.

She tucked the final sample into her specimen storage container so that it would stay just as fresh when she handed it over to Jeoh as it had been the day she had collected it. There, it nestled comfortably among the others she had gathered and she looked at the vials thoughtfully as she wondered, not for the first time and unlikely for the last, what they would be used for. Just as every other time, she failed to come up with any viable theories. The only thing she knew for certain was that she had collected enough to meet his quota.

"I have your samples," she said on the comm once he picked up. "The permission form is ready as well."

"Understood. Please stand by." Had she not known better, she would have believed the voice on the other end to have been a recorded message, it was so devoid of inflection. Not that she actually did know better, of course. The message was so generic it could easily have been recorded.

Pressure mounted in her head, not strongly enough to cause any pain, probably not even strongly enough to be noticed by someone who hadn't ever practiced with psionic abilities, but it was glaringly obvious to her. She was being scanned.

She whirled around, searching for the source of the scan, and almost tripped over Jeoh. He had appeared directly behind her, almost within arm's reach. As quickly as he had arrived, the pressure in her skull dissipated.

"Was that you?" she demanded, incensed at the intrusion. "We had an agreement; you wouldn't poke around in my head." She stepped closer until she was almost pressed physically against him. "That was the deal we made, that you agreed to. If I can't even trust you on this, then the deal's off. I don't need someone I can't trust.

He raised both hands defensively against her ire although he showed no additional signals of distress at her reaction. "All I needed was to see where you were so that I could arrive in the correct location. I dug no further than that, you have my word."

Uncertain on how far she could trust his word, despite Gazer's assurance that he would do as he said, she eyed him with blatant suspicion for a long moment before settling once more. Even if he had broken his word, there was nothing she could do to stop him.

Not, at least, until her abilities were restored.

As she calmed, another surprising realization struck her. She, as did many other psionists, specialized in mental abilities that allowed her to find, read, and even modify or place thoughts and memories in the mind of another sentient being. Hers was not the only area of expertise, as others spent their time focused on travel, which allowed them to journey to distant places without the benefit of a ship or the delays involved in interstellar travel. Both types of ability took many years, the majority of a lifetime for some species, in order to become functional and usable. For the abilities to be fully mastered took a great deal longer. For him to be able to appear in her location after scanning her mind to determine where that location was, he had to have spent a great deal of time developing both of the abilities, either simultaneously or concurrently.

Either way, that amount of training would take a great deal of time, time most beings simply didn't have before dying of old age.

Just how old was this man?

# CHAPTER 11

# ASSISTANCE REQUEST

---

"It is only a matter of time, as I am sure you understand." The Qadar on the screen was visibly frustrated, although trying his best to not show it. "Their force moves closer by the day. If nothing is done to stop them, they will be upon us."

It had been some time since Ryan Moore had seen the speaker for the Voivode Council in such a state. While he could understand his predicament, there was little he could do to quell his fears. "We are also concerned about their latest movements," he explained, "but there is little we can do. We are also under orders to remain in our current position."

"But you are the military branch! How can you just stand by and watch this happen?" Shuja Caolan stopped speaking, closed his eyes, and took a calming breath. "We are still fighting off the A.T. military and we are losing ground to them by the day. This new threat only adds to the danger we face. If the two teams join forces, assuming they haven't already, there will be almost nothing we can do to maintain our stand against them."

Ryan truly felt for their situation. Only ten years previously, the conversation wouldn't have been needed at all, as his men would have already joined the fight in defense of Onoquoi, one of their oldest allies. However, that was before he had signed that level of freedom away by joining the Interplanetary Government. "Have you spoken to the Interplanetary

Government?" he asked. "I'm sure that if they knew the situation, they would be willing to allow us to come help."

"We have tried that. Multiple times, we have tried that. We asked them for assistance when A.T. threatened to enter our space, we asked them for assistance when they crossed our borders. We asked for help when half of our defensive troops were engaged with the fight and we asked for help when those numbers dropped to a third. Nothing was done. Now, seeing that the Iron Gauntlet approaches and knowing the damage they have done to other systems, we have asked for assistance once again. We have asked, we have asked more times than I am able to count, and we have been rejected each time. Most recently, we have been explicitly instructed to make no contact with you in regards to this matter. Why have you become unwilling to help us? Have we offended you in some way? If so, please let us know so that we can put it to rights."

Although he showed no outward signs of it, Ryan's blood had begun to boil at the Qadar speaker's words. While he had been tracing the movements of A.T. into Qadar territory, he had been instructed quite clearly that his troops were not needed in the battle, that the Qadar would take care of it themselves. Now, it appeared that he had been lied to.

Even worse, it appeared that there were forces at play that were actively keeping Triad from their core function. Worse still, it was giving the appearance that Triad was at fault for their lack of response.

"We have also requested to aide you and your people in this," he explained. "What you are telling me today is at complete odds from what we had been told." He took a drink of his coffee, surreptitiously checking to ensure that the line upon which he and Shuja spoke was still secure. Despite the lack of findings after Diamond's stunt, wherein she re-routed the call to appear it had originated in Ryan's own office, he was still concerned about comm security. The last thing he needed was to have others listening in on their conversation. "Now that I know the truth, that our assistance has been requested, I need to figure out how we can help you without violating our current agreements."

Shuja Caolan breathed an audible sigh of relief on the other end of the comm. "Thank you," he said simply. "That is all I ask. That is all I had ever asked for. I had thought that we had offended you in some way that we were unaware and you had merely been unwilling to assist us."

"That would never be the case," Ryan stressed. "You know as well as any that we are here for the sole purpose of safeguarding those around us. That has been our mission since our inception and there has never been any reason to change that." He took another drink of his beverage, needing to double-check the security of the line yet again. "Our relationship with your people is sound, no offense has been given to my knowledge. Even had offense been given, that wouldn't stop us from coming to help you and your people." He had no doubts that the line was secure and would stay that way but was willing to take absolutely no chances. Although his conversation with the speaker of the Voivode Council did not yet violate any of his agreements with the Interplanetary Government, it was growing steadily closer to doing precisely that.

"Our current contract prohibits us from getting involved directly until we are given the authorization by the Interplanetary Government which, at this time, it does not appear that we will be getting any time soon. I am sure you're already aware of this."

"We are. But there must be something you can do."

"What I can do is to send aid by means of supplies to you. That is simple enough and does not violate any of our agreements."

"Supplies?" Dismay added weight to the word. "We need no supplies. What we need are troops, trained fighters to bolster the defensive line. We need someone to go on the offensive, to drive them back."

"I understand that. But what I intend to do is to send you supplies. I ask only that you trust me for the moment and believe me when

I say that you will be very pleased with the supplies I intend to send you." He hoped that his voice, tone, and word choice passed the message along so that he didn't have to explain his plan explicitly. Even on a secure line, one still needed to maintain a level of reservation in what was said. Triad may have hired the best communication security team they could find but that didn't detract from others doing the same thing, potentially even better than his own men had done. The Queen of Diamonds had proven that quite clearly.

"That is all I can ask." Shuja settled at his words, apparently either comprehending the unspoken message or just trusting in Ryan. "I maintain my concerns, particularly since it appears that they are preparing for a pincer attack. If their intentions are such, they will breach what little defenses we still have both quickly and easily."

"Your suspicions on that appear to be founded," Ryan admitted, "but the supplies I am sending you should help to alleviate some of their potential for success."

"All right them. I shall eagerly await these supplies of yours."

As Ryan ended the call, he had to forcibly restrain himself from throwing his coffee cup, smashing it against a wall in his office. "What in the hells are they playing at?" Antsy and agitated, he settled the threatened cup down carefully, got up from his desk and paced back and forth across the width of his office. Frustration balled his hands into fists as he replayed the conversation in his mind once more.

"I take it the call didn't go well?" Brian Coffee asked as he stepped quietly into the room, fresh cup of coffee in hand.

"The Qadar have been members of the Interplanetary Government far longer than we have. If they had asked for assistance, why wasn't it sent? Why were we told to stand down if the Voivode Council explicitly asked us to come?" Commander Moore held his own personal integrity at the highest level and insisted that the men and women who answered to him carried themselves with similar regard.

For even a hint that he had simply decided to not assist the Qadar, for someone to lead them to the belief that he lacked the moral fortitude to aid them when they needed it the most galled him to his very core and offended every fiber of his being. It was the single greatest insult that could have been levied against him at that moment and he was unwilling to let it rest. He eyed the cup as it was placed onto his desk. "I really don't think I need any more caffeine right now."

"I know," Coffee agreed amicably. "That's why I brought you decaffeinated."

Ryan stopped and chuckled. He should have known that his assistant would know which type of coffee to bring him.

"If I understand the situation correctly, the Interplanetary Government has blocked your assistance to the Qadar, despite their membership and direct request for aid. Is that correct?"

Ryan scowled as he took a drink of the coffee. "Yeah, that's how it sounds, at least. Either that or someone is doing a damn good job of making it look that way."

"So what do you intend to do about it?"

"I intend," Ryan explained, "to follow our contract to the letter. While we are contracted to the Interplanetary Government, I cannot send military aid until official authorization is granted to do such by them. The way things stand right now, I don't think that authorization will be given anytime soon, if at all." He set the cup back on his desk and looked at it thoughtfully. "What I can do is to send aid in the form of supplies."

Coffee tilted his head slightly to the side. "I can't imagine the Qadar need much by way of supplies. How is sending them something they don't need going to help?"

Commander Moore had been in charge of Triad for a very long time, far longer than anyone, Ryan included, had ever expected. One of the reasons for that was due to his strategic mind, which allowed him to plan further in advance than most people could, with plenty of contingencies as well in the all-to-often situation where a primary plan, or even one of its many contingencies, failed. From a strategic standpoint, his continued placement as leader of Triad was the most sensible. That amount of time had also allowed him to build strong relationships among the other cultures and world leaders across the galaxy, which further allowed him to request and perform favors that strengthened not only Triad's position but also the positions of their allies. It was that relationship that had almost been damaged through Triad's inaction, which inevitably fell onto Ryan's shoulders.

Those years and relationships also gave him the experience to understand how others would react in response to his actions, which only increased the accuracy of his planning sessions. But the greatest and most widespread reason that Ryan had been Triad's commander for so long was because his people demanded it. That demand was a direct result of not just his strategic skill and diplomatic relationships, but the trust and faith that everyone placed in him, trust and faith that had been earned and reinforced over the years. Trust and faith that he placed a high value on, knowing full well how hard that trust had been earned and how easily the decisions he made could cause everyone to lose faith in him.

That reputation, the most valuable asset that he possessed, was once again being put to the test by the apparently deliberate withholding of Triad support by the Interplanetary Government. "The supplies themselves are irrelevant," he explained. "I won't be sending much because you are correct; they don't need supplies. What they do need is a strong showing of our support, enough to convince A.T. and the Iron Gauntlet that they are not solely standing against the Voivode Council, that they are standing against Triad as well." He smiled and took another drink of his decaffeinated coffee.

Another, less well-known reason that many people, particularly people outside of Triad, continued to support Ryan's leadership was his willingness to bend the rules when he felt it was absolutely necessary. While he may be against outright breaking them, he recognized that there were times when flexibility was warranted. Some had criticized his willingness to do so but appreciation and approval were far more common. He already knew, had known since early in his conversation with Shuja Caolan, that this was a time where he needed to be both strategic and creative.

"I see." Over the years, Coffee had come to recognize when his commander was up to a plan and could usually follow along with his unspoken ideas. "Might I suggest an addition to this plan of yours?"

"What's that?"

"I was talking with a friend not too long ago. Apparently there is to be a rather large exposition on Onoquoi, showing off their latest technologies. If we had anything that you might want to add to the display, I am certain that they would be interested in seeing some of our latest equipment."

Ryan looked at his assistant thoughtfully. "I heard about that too," he admitted, "but I'd forgotten. You're absolutely correct, I've never seen anyone turn down the opportunity to get a closer look at what we've got out in the field.

I'd just need to find something that wasn't still considered classified, something that is safe to put on display." He chuckled again. "This just makes the whole plan that much simpler.

"There is absolutely nothing in our contract that states supplies must be delivered by a supply ship or cargo transport."

# ADVANCING POSITION

---

"How in the hell did this happen?" Bryck stormed from one end of the room to the next, repressing the urge to put his fist violently through a wall. The former Ace no longer wore the trademark shaped crystal lapel pin, having left it behind when he abandoned the Deck to help form the Iron Gauntlet. His new uniform held no insignia of rank but none were needed. Everyone knew who was in charge. "The Cardiss base should have been perfectly secure."

The base on Cardiss, the crowning glory of the Deck's resources, had been perfectly positioned to defeat any and all attempts to enter. Every aspect of the base had been carefully chosen to provide the utmost security and defense, an impenetrable fortress for its residents. It hovered above the surface of the planet on which it had been placed, maintaining power through its own energy supply. Even the oxygen that allowed the inhabitants to breathe was self-contained to ensure that no contaminants could be introduced to sicken the Cards or to cause an evacuation. The Queen of Diamonds, the original leader of the Deck, had chosen and set up the base brilliantly. Just as she had done with every other plan she made. There had been only a handful of changes needed to the defense systems after her departure and most of those had been due to personal choice rather than necessity. "We had the latest technology in that place, the most un-hackable system ever created. So how, someone please tell me, did that half-breed manage to get through it all?"

"We're not sure," one of his attendants nervously answered. "We think that someone on the inside must have overridden the security measures. I have a team investigating now."

"Impossible. The only person who had the override codes was me." That had been a deliberate decision on his part. Even the idiot King of Clubs, as many times as he had demanded override codes of his own, had been denied them. There had never been a time when the inept puppet would have needed that level of access. Figureheads don't need control, they just need to play their parts. At least the King of Clubs had done that part correctly. Few had suspected the real power behind the throne. At least, few who cared to admit their suspicions.

"As far as we can tell, the core system lost all power during the attack. Its backup systems never kicked on."

"You're telling me," Bryck turned on his

minion in fury, "that we had the most advanced technology in the galaxy, technology that most governments don't even have access to, and someone just TURNED IT OFF?" The calm and cool demeanor he had shown, so carefully maintained the whole time he had acted in the guise of a loyal Ace, had disappeared when he heard the full extent of what had transpired at Cardiss. The final vestiges of self-restraint had disappeared as the news grew worse with every conversation.

"It may have been something to do with that unusual weapon she deployed," another added. "We still don't know what it was."

"That had to have been Knave's doing. He's the only one who had the ability to create a weapon of that caliber."

"I'm still surprised Diamond allowed it to be used. We all know her views on killing anyone."

"That didn't stop her from killing the Aces we sent to apprehend her."

"True, but I thought that was just her acting

defensively. The attack on the Cardiss base was definitely offensive."

"Nothing should have been able to breach those shields, particularly not an energy weapon." The weapon unleashed on Cardiss had been truly devastating. In one shot, it had completely taken every system offline. "Are we certain it wasn't an EMP burst?"

"It was not. Even had they used an EMP, the base was completely shielded against it."

"Then what the hell was it?" The former Ace demanded once more.

"We think," yet another aide spoke up, his voice much smaller than the others had been, "she may have gotten her hands on the Blood-hound virus."

That stopped everyone in their tracks and all eyes focused on the speaker. "The Blood-hound virus," one finally said. "Are you certain of this?"

"No, but it's the best theory we've come up with so far. Most of the results of that attack seemed very similar to what the virus was re-ported to do the last time it was unleashed."

"No it wasn't," one of the others protested. "None of the airlocks were opened. We all got off safely. If this was the Bloodhound virus, it would have killed all of us."

"I didn't say it *was* the Bloodhound virus, I said it was *like* it. It may have been a next-generation version of the virus, designed to be less lethal to everyone on the station."

"The only ones who have access to that," the first speaker pointed out, "is Triad. If this was based on the Bloodhound virus, that can only mean that Triad's involved now."

"We're screwed," the timid aide pointed out. "If Triad's after us, there's no way we're strong enough to hold out against them."

"They're not involved," Bryck said simply. "I have ensured that they will stay clear of this." He took a deep breath, trying to regain some of his composure. He still had an organization to run, after all. That would be near impossible if he didn't even have control over himself.

"I still blame the Zoscarians," the first aide spoke up once more. "Had they gotten rid of the pesky Queen when we told them about her, none of this would have happened."

"Very true," Bryck agreed. "And that oversight hasn't been forgotten. But we have bigger things to deal with right now." He had personally ensured that the Zoscarian government had been informed that the Queen of Diamonds intended to relieve them of their royal regalia, he had even assisted with the plan for stopping her from escaping with the goods. Once he received confirmation that she and Knave had been destroyed, he began his takeover of the Deck. A takeover that had worked beautifully.

Until, of course, the Queen returned. As it turned out, she was far less dead than he had been led to believe. And far angrier as well.

He should have known better than to trust Zoscarian intelligence. But that was a matter he could deal with at a later time. He had more important things to address at the moment.

At least he'd had the foresight to place that foolish Tet in place as king, he realized. Had he taken the overt leadership of the Deck, he would likely be dead at that moment as well. Instead, he and those closest to him had been forced to hide out in a quiet corner of the galaxy, pulling in those who remained loyal to their cause and waiting for the Iron Gauntlet to be complete. Not quite the grand resurgence he had envisioned but far better than the worst-case option. Now he just needed the final handful of pieces to fall into place so that he could begin the next phase of his scheme.

That day had finally arrived. "Bring me the expansion plans."

"We have a lead on the Qadar defense network." The timid aide switched on the bank of monitors, which showed the layout of their target system. "It is well hidden but unguarded, so we should be able to access it as soon as we finish tracing the current location of the access codes."

"Excellent. How long will that trace take?"

"Not long. Expect that we will have access within the month. We have confirmed who has the codes, so now it's just a question of acquiring them."

Considering how dangerous the array was, he was surprised that it hadn't been kept more secure. That made part of his plan a lot simpler, assuming the intel was correct. "Those codes have to be heavily guarded. What kind of defenses are we anticipating?"

"Surprisingly few. It appears that the Onoquoi government is unaware of the location and has taken no steps to defend them against us."

Finally. Something was going right. He sat down in one of the leather chairs and steepled his fingers on the table, resting his chin on his fingertips. "You said you know who has the codes. Have you located this person? When can we expect to have them in our possession?"

"We have. A team has already begun working toward gaining them."

"Once we have the codes, how much longer before we gain full control?"

"We still need to access the facility where the system is housed. Once we have that and we gain the codes, not long at all. If all goes according to plan, we will gain complete control over the entire Onoquoi territory within the year."

The former Ace smiled. Six years of planning, searching for the legendary weapon system, the most powerful weapon he could have even dreamed of, was about to come to fruition. He was so close; he could almost taste the victory.

Nothing could stop him now.

# BACKGROUND CHECK

Gazer did not appreciate the appeal of a good mystery. She didn't enjoy the search, she didn't enjoy the chase, and she definitely didn't enjoy the unknown pitfalls that invariably resulted of the unknown. Despite her lack of enjoyment, or perhaps because of it, she happened to be quite good at uncovering things other people wanted to keep hidden. Very little happened within her range of influence about which she remained unaware and, due in no small part to the allowances granted her by Triad, her range extended to far greater distances than most were aware. Ally or foe, if they stored their information on a computer, sooner or later she would have access to it.

Most mysteries were of little ultimate consequence. Generally, they consisted of small lies to hide uncomfortable truths, hidden caches of weapons or trade goods in case the wars came back again. Those types of mysteries didn't bother her overly much, but the bigger ones bothered her a great deal. Recently, a particularly obnoxious mystery had landed in her lap, one she was determined to get to the bottom of.

The mystery about the weapon used by the Queen of Diamonds and Knave of Spades had been easy enough to solve. By tracing their movements back to the planet upon which they had been stranded, she had been able to piece together the truth of the weapon including the components used to build it and how it worked. All of that information had been compiled into a thorough and comprehensive report, complete with recommendations for defense against such a weapon in the future, and was currently sitting on Commander Moore's desk. A second report, similar but much smaller in scope, had been passed along to Tripp and Mike and the rest of the leadership at World Industries. As far as Gazer was concerned, there was nothing more to know about that.

She was satisfied.

It had been due to this distaste for mysteries that had brought her existence and skills to Triad's attention in the first place. Back when she was still young, chronologically speaking, her planet had not been a part of the Interplanetary Government. They hadn't even been aware that other life existed in the galaxy, although many had suspected as much. That world had been remarkably similar in their galactic knowledge to the world Diamond and Knave had been stranded on for so long. Just as she was now, Gazer had been highly interested in knowing what others had been up to, particularly others within her own government. Not that she ever did anything with the information, she had simply wanted to know. During one of her occasional forays into computer systems that were not as secure as they were believed to be, she had uncovered evidence of someone else doing the same thing. Back-tracing their route, she had encountered an almost-unsurmountable firewall, one that had stymied her for weeks. Getting through that firewall had been both her biggest achievement and her biggest life-changer to date.

She hadn't realized, of course, that the others spying on her government were not even from her planet. Far from the international spies she had believed them to be, the others had been Triad agents. As soon as she entered their computer system, however, they knew about her. Suspecting that she had been placed on the planet as a sleeper agent by one of their enemies, so certain had they been that none of the planet's inhabitants should have been able to find or trace them, troops had been deployed, taking her into custody with the rest of her own planet's residents none the wiser. Questioning had been stressful and exhausting, often performed by people who didn't look anything like the people to whom she was accustomed. Finally satisfied that she was simply exceptionally talented with computers, they had offered her a choice: she could return to her life, free and clear, or she could come to work for them.

Once her fear had subsided and she discovered all that the intergalactic military had to offer, she hadn't looked back.

Now, unfortunately, she had a new mystery to solve.

"No luck yet?" DJ poked his head in through the door to check on her. "You've been at it for a while now."

DJ was one of the biggest determining factors in her decision to remain with Triad. He was one of the people she met during those first few weeks, as his team had been the one to capture her. They had quickly formed a friendship, one that had grown over her period of training that allowed her to be field-ready. When she had been assigned to his unit, both were relieved that there were no prohibitions about dating coworkers. Nor were there any prohibitions about marrying them.

"I know," she sighed. "I actually finished what I was working on before but now I have something new to noodle at."

"New?" he walked in and perched on the edge of her desk. "What did you find now?"

"It's about M'Tarl." she explained. "Even Galeah came by to talk about her. She's concerned about all of this and I have to admit that I'm a bit worried too."

"What's there to worry about? She's pretty highly trained, even by our standards."

"Oh, I'm not worried about that. At least, not exactly. But anyone who can take a person's abilities away like that? Now that is something I'm very worried about."

DJ nodded knowingly. "Worried it could happen to you one day?"

"Yes. No. Not exactly." She sighed again. "Even if someone wanted to, I really doubt they'd be able to get close enough to do something like that to me. But I also know that I'm a pretty high-value target. Mouse too. Am I directly concerned that we could lose our abilities? No. But do I want to know how it happened so I can stop it just in case someone else gets targeted? Absolutely."

"You and Mouse aren't the only psionists out there, not even the only ones in Triad. There are plenty of targets who aren't as protected as the two of you are."

"There's another part of this too, one that has me curious."

"That's not good." DJ knew more than anyone about the peril of Gazer's curiosity. "What are you curious about?"

"M'Tarl herself. There's got to be a reason this happened to her. So now I'm wondering what about her was so dangerous that someone had felt it necessary to take her abilities from her." She scowled. "I mean, I don't think she's actually dangerous, not in the traditional sense and not to any of us. But there's got to be a reason she was targeted."

"I can understand that. So... want to tell me what you've found so far?"

"Well, first of all, she's officially a class two, right? At least, she was before this whole mess started." When DJ nodded, she shook her head. "There's no way she's a class two. She's probably at least a three, but I'd put money on a four."

DJ cocked his head and looked at her. "Why would someone register as a two if they were actually a four? That doesn't make much sense." A person's power and skills determined what level they were. Two was pretty average for a person with standard power levels and routine training on how to use their abilities. A psionist with a higher power level could charge more for their services and were much higher in demand than those with lower levels.

She tapped one of her fingernails against her bottom lip for a moment before answering. "Well, it kind of does. If someone wanted to keep up the appearance that they were less powerful, less of a threat, I could see them registering a lot lower. Considering what she does for a living, well what she did, it makes an amount of sense to keep a low profile. I'm sure her superiors in the Voivode Council knew her true power levels."

"Why do you think she's higher than that?"

She turned one of the monitors toward him. Displayed on the screen was one of M'Tarl's brain scans. "I got this from the hospital, it was taken on her last visit. On the area here, it shows a lot of activity. I mean a lot. More than what a class two should be displaying." She pointed to a section of the screen. "This is closer to what my own scans look like in this area. Not quite as high, so I know she's not above a five, but way more than enough for just a level two."

DJ peered closer at the scan. "So what were they looking for in there?"

Gazer answered through gritted teeth. "That's the question, now isn't it? I have no idea." This was hardly the first time she had needed to uncover secret information about someone who had come into contact with Triad, often involving the use of multiple identities. About a year previously, she had been tasked with just such an assignment regarding the Queen of Diamonds, after she had made direct contact with Commander Moore. In that instance, Gazer had been unable to uncover her true identity, a fact that continued to bother her, but she had been able to unearth enough of the woman's history to determine that she was not a threat to Ryan or anyone else in Triad.

Now there was another person who had been in contact with not only Gazer's own team on multiple occasions but had also infiltrated Galeah's social group, the Gossip, as well. "It's only a matter of time before an official background request comes in on her," she explained, "so I might as well get started already."

"Well, don't take too long," DJ said as he stood and stretched. "Dinner's almost done and you've hardly eaten anything today."

"What time is it?" She glanced at the clock, surprised by how late it had gotten already. "Okay. I'll be down shortly."

Once he was gone, she turned back to her monitors. She had already begun to trace M'Tarl's history, which ended abruptly thirty-five years previously. Or rather, she corrected herself, it started abruptly at that time. Before that date, there was absolutely no record of M'Tarl Nox anywhere in the galaxy.

Visually speaking, it made sense that M'Tarl may have simply been a very young Qadar, but Gazer didn't believe that for a second. The woman simply had too much knowledge in her eyes. "She's definitely seen more than thirty-five years of life."

"Maybe she just changed her name back then," she mused. Name changes were generally easy enough to trace but occasionally someone forgot to file all of the appropriate documentation in the correct place, making traceability harder than it needed to be. If that was all this was, she could rest easily. Heck, she might even be done with it before dinner was ready.

That hope ended as quickly as it began, which was no surprise whatsoever to Gazer.

No name change applications were on file anywhere, nor were there any signals of a less authorized change of identity. Nobody had disappeared or died suddenly without reasonable explanation around that time, leading her to yet another dead end. Undaunted but growing more annoyed at her own inability to uncover the truth, she kept digging. It was quickly becoming a mystery and she simply wasn't in the mood.

"Dinner's done." A massive bushel of blue hair announced Troll's arrival. As always, it stood straight up out of his head, a feat Gazer still didn't know how he achieved. At least he wore clothes this time, she realized. More often than not, he preferred to spend his time in the nude.

"Yeah, I'll be down soon."

Troll chuckled. "No, you won't. You've got that look in your eye again."

She finally looked up at him. "What look?"

"The look that says you're not coming down to dinner." He stepped forward and placed a plate on the edge of her desk. "But I'm amazing, so I brought it to you instead."

She blinked at the food for a moment, almost not recognizing what the plate was for. "Thanks," she said finally. "And you're right, I probably wouldn't be down soon."

He stood next to her desk, staring at her expectantly, until she stopped working long enough to take a few bites of the meal. Once he confirmed that she would eat something, Troll nodded in satisfaction and withdrew.

While she was taking a break, she sent a quick email to one of her company's directors. StarrTech, the computer company she had founded shortly after joining Triad, had been tasked with the final testing for the latest brain jack design and she needed an update. There were already teams waiting in line to get theirs for final field testing and she wanted to ensure the testing was going smoothly.

Once the food was gone and all necessary emails had been sent, she returned to her research. Just under two hours later, she found something interesting.

Sometimes, she realized with dismay, interesting was even worse than mysterious.

# JEOH'S NEWS

---

"There doesn't seem to be anyone here," Jeoh commented once he arrived and looked around.

They were standing on a plain, coated with tall grasses and low scrub brushes as far as the eye could see, with the barest hint of flowers peeking through to enjoy the meager sunlight. It was spring on the planet M'Tarl had chosen, her favorite season of them all. A low wind

gusted past, teasing at the grasses and causing them to dance and sway. No birds flew by
overhead but a scant handful of clouds drifted
along, guided by the stronger winds higher in
the atmosphere. Her original choice for meeting locations had recently suffered flooding
from an unexpected influx of seasonal rain-
fall, so this had been her secondary option,
a decision she didn't regret in the slightest.
While the ship she spent the majority of her
time within was always comfortably warm,
there was something to be said about the de-
lightful spring breeze and the scents it carried
with it. As an added bonus, the planet she had
selected was barren of intelligent life, so her
lack of abilities didn't cause her any added
distress that could take away her enjoyment
from the experience.

M'Tarl reluctantly tore her eyes away from
the landscape to view the man. "Is that a problem?" She pushed a stray length of hair out of
her face and tucked it behind an ear. The wind
immediately caught it once more and sent it
dancing.

"Not at all. I hadn't expected to arrive in an uninhabited area, that's all." Unlike her, he appeared to pay no attention whatsoever to the environment in which they stood, his attention focused directly and intently on her.

M'Tarl handed him the requested writ and watched as he carefully read through it. His brows lowered as he nodded slowly, in apparent agreement with her terms. She tried to read his expression but there was nothing much to read. Other than the lowered brows, he was as blank as always. "You don't seem pleased with this. I'd expected you to be happier."

"It will suffice." He tucked the document into a pocket within his jacket. "I hadn't expected it to be as explicitly written as it is but you certainly were thorough." He looked up to meet her eyes once more, his brows again neutral. "An agreement is an agreement and it is precisely what I requested." His expression changed slightly before he added, "I've never had anyone put an expiration date on one of these before. For you to think of that is quite impressive."

Not sure whether she took that as a compliment or not, M'Tarl turned back to the business at hand. There was something slightly different about Jeoh, something she couldn't quite put her finger on. He looked just the same as he had previously but something about him just felt off. "I have the samples here for you," she said as she opened the containment unit to show him. "Ten genetic samples, all from different systems, none of which were on your list."

"Wonderful." He looked genuinely pleased to see them as she handed them over. "And you've even labeled from where each was taken."

"You seemed to want them catalogued," she explained, "so I figured it would be easiest for you if I recorded that." It sounded plausible but hadn't been her true reason for labeling each of the samples. She wanted no room for argument on whether they had been correctly collected, or that they were not from acceptable planets. One thing she had learned quite effectively during her time with the Voivode

Council was that the best way one could win an argument was to ensure that nothing remained about which could be argued. Many of the contacts she had worked with had been just as devious as Jeoh, with equally mysterious motivations.

"As I should have expected," he smiled once more as he tucked the samples into the same pocket as where he had stored the writ. "Your reputation for thoroughness precedes you."

"I have a reputation?" M'Tarl didn't like the sound of that. She shouldn't have been surprised that he had looked into her before this meeting but his statement still took her aback. She generally went out of her way to be as forgettable and unremarkable as possible. The idea of something as innocuous-sounding as a reputation could grow into a huge problem in her line of work.

"Not to most people," he reassured her, "but, then again, I'm not exactly most people."

"No, I suppose you aren't." She looked at him askance. "Why do you look different today?"

He raised a single eyebrow as he looked at her from the corner of an eye. "What do you mean by that?"

"I can't quite put my finger on it but something about you looks different from the last time I saw you."

"Oh," he tucked the writ into a pocket. "That. Yes, some people tend to notice, although most don't. You are, as I expected, highly observant."

"So you do look different." It was a statement, not a question.

"No. I do not look any different today than I have on any other day. Your confusion and perceived change in my appearance stem from the fact that today is the first day you have seen me."

Her brows lowered and she blinked at him. "Come again?" No matter how she rolled his words around in her head, they failed to make any sense.

"The simple explanation is that I am a clone. A copy made based off of my original form. Were you unaware of this?"

"A clone? But cloning is highly restricted. How did you get cloned?"

"Technically, the me with whom you met the last time was a clone as well. Nobody has seen my original form in a very long time."

"He was a clone too? How many of you are there? And where is the original? Why has it been so long since he has been seen?" Questions, many more than just the ones that escaped her mouth, rocketed around in her head.

"I, as in the original Jeoh, have been imprisoned for a great many years. I am not allowed to roam about freely as you are but my knowledge was deemed too valuable to keep locked away."

"So they cloned you?"

He chuckled. "No. I had already begun making clones of myself, but that reason, particularly when combined with the fact that cloning is legal in the portion of the galaxy where my original body is being held, was the allowance needed by the Interplanetary Government to allow the continued existence of my clones." His voice faded at that and he appeared to start listening intently at a sound that was inaudible to M'Tarl.

She knew most of the parts of the galaxy reasonably well, at least well enough to know the high-level laws in each sector. There were only a handful of places where cloning was still legal, most of which were under A. T. control. The idea that Jeoh, or at least the original version of him, had been A.T. was one that she couldn't dismiss the possibility about offhand. Remembering some of the stories she had heard about the man before meeting him, the possibility seemed much less far-fetched than she had once thought. She had known he was dangerous, any who had ever heard of him knew that much about the enigmatic man, but she hadn't ever heard so much as a rumor that there was more than one of him. If he had been A.T, that could easily explain why he had been allowed to make clones and why he was deemed too dangerous to allow free roam of the galaxy.

"I have news," he turned to face her again, his eyes focused once more.

"What was that?" she interrupted. "I have pretty good hearing but I didn't hear a thing."

"That's because it was an internal communication. I received an update on your test results from the clones back home."

Her mind had already been whirling and his latest statement wasn't making things any easier. "Clones back home? How many of you are there?"

"That is not important now. The important part is that I have uncovered an unusual compound in your system."

"What kind of unusual compound?" She wasn't too worried, as most of the compounds she encountered on a regular basis could be considered unusual. Further, his strange manner of referring to both himself and the other clones was giving her a headache. Did they all share one personality? Were they actually a hive mind, similar to how some species of bees and ants shared a common consciousness? Who, precisely, had locked him away?

He had mentioned the Interplanetary Government, but not in relation to his incarceration. What had he done to require such a sentence? Was he actually a larger threat to her than she had originally expected? Was all of this an enormous mistake on her part?

"I'm not sure that this compound caused the blockage in your psionic abilities but it likely played a part."

"So what is it?"

"I'm not quite sure, at least not precisely. It has some characteristics that strongly resemble one I've seen before. The structures within it are similar in form and composition to those found in a drug called ZB-2. Are you familiar with it.?

"ZB-2?" She thought about it for a moment. As a part of her training, she had been administered an assortment of compounds, primarily consisting of vaccinations against diseases that were known throughout the galaxy but which hadn't been widespread on her home world. That was common practice among field agents to minimize the risk when encountering contaminants to which they hadn't naturally gotten a resistance already. When she asked if one of those inoculations could be the source, he shook his head.

"This is definitely not something you would have been given as a part of a vaccination battery. This is more akin to something that would be taken..." he looked around the clearing as though seeking inspiration. "Recreationally."

"Rec... no. I don't take anything like that recreationally." She didn't even like taking freely available pain-relieving medications, the very idea of taking some sort of illicit drug went completely against her nature. She required a sharp mind and sharper reflexes. Recreational drugs resulted in the opposite of that.

"I hadn't expected as much. But it was worth mentioning. People do tend to surprise on occasion, after all."

"That's true enough. So you think that this drug has something to do with my psionics?" She thought back to the interrogation that had caused the whole mess, trying to recall whether anything was administered to her in the process. She couldn't remember having been given anything, and she definitely wouldn't have taken it willingly if it had been offered, which left only a couple of options. First, it was something that one of the implements used against her had been tainted with. Second, it had been administered once she lost consciousness. She wasn't sure which of those ideas bothered her the most.

"I'm not positive on anything yet. Until I get a sample of the drug to compare against the compound found in the sample taken from you, there is little else I will be able to tell you."

"But can you fix it without the drug?"

He shook his head sadly. "Without a sample of the drug, there is very little I can do. Until I am able to confirm whether or not it is even the same compound, I will not be able to work on your restorative."

M'Tarl sighed. She should have known this wouldn't be easy. Nothing in her life had been easy even when she had maintained her psionics, so why should now be any different?

"So now I need to go find a sample of this drug. Excellent." She had never trafficked in drugs and didn't have the slightest clue where to start. Until that portion of their conversation, she'd never even heard of the drug. "I suppose you'll want to go with me?"

"Of course." He smiled his unnatural smile once more and tapped the pocket where he had placed the writ. "Where you go, I go as well."

"Or one of you, at least." She wondered whether the writ actually extended to all of his clones or if it only allowed one at a time to be at her side. While she was sure that more of his clones would rotate in and out, likely often without her being any the wiser about the exchange, she hoped that his presence remained limited. There had been no limitation on how many of him could accompany her, as she had no clue that level of detail would have been necessary. What other surprises remained up his sleeves, she wondered. "This had better work."

# ILLICIT ACQUISITION

Finding an illicit drug, M'Tarl discovered, was nowhere near as easy as it had initially seemed it would be. Her first attempts to locate a source of the drug had proven much more difficult than anticipated, as the supply had recently been severely decreased. "Considering how many people across the galaxy are addicted to this stuff," she commented to Jeoh after yet another failed attempt to locate a ZB-2 supplier, "you'd think it would be easier to find."

"We did find something," he pointed out, "so it's not a total loss."

His words were accurate. While she had expected to have some difficulty finding the drug, she hadn't expected as much difficulty as she'd found. "How can there be so many people using it when there isn't any out there to buy?" They had found that the drug in question could only still be easily found in a handful of areas, none of which were ones with which she was very familiar. "I really don't like the Tyrannus system," she sighed.

"Is that where this happened?" He tapped the side of his head with one long bony fingertip as he asked.

"No." She sat at her console and activated the panel, beginning the warmup process for the engines. "That happened somewhere else." His eyes showed that he didn't quite believe her but at least he didn't press the issue. Despite no longer being an active member of the Voivode Council, she wasn't interested in giving away any of their secrets. While she wasn't certain that the location of her latest assignment was classified, that wasn't a risk she wanted to take. She still held faith that if she was to play her cards in just the right way, she might be able to get her position back. A long shot at best, she understood, but it was worth the effort. To that end, she had no intention of doing anything that could jeopardize her acceptability to the council.

"Strange that the Tyrannians are responsible for this new drug," Jeoh said as he buckled himself in. "I wouldn't have expected anything this advanced out of them."

"I really doubt it's the Tyrannians manufacturing it. They've never been interested in chemicals before, so I can't think of anything that would lead them to develop one now." As far as she was aware, the people who lived on the single inhabited planet of the Tyrannian system were some of the least technologically advanced in all of the galaxy, at least as far as sentient species went. Their knowledge of science had only barely advanced to the exploration of their own world and a rudimentary exploration of their moons. "It's probably based on one of the uninhabited planets, maybe a planetary base or a space station that the locals don't know about." The low rumble of engines on standby power changed to a higher, deeper whine as the drives flared to life and she released the docking clamps, dropping the small vehicle into empty space so that she could leave the station.

As they flew toward the edge of the solar system, she looked askance at her erstwhile passenger. She still didn't understand much at all about the man sitting next to her. Despite all of the warnings she had heard about him, all the legends that had been told, she had no clue as to who he really was. Nobody had ever even hinted at the idea that he was a clone and reports of his abilities seemed to be too fanciful to be believed. Of course, she had already seen him perform feats that were beyond belief, as his ability to both mind scan and to teleport was one of the most impressive things she had seen in a long time. "What were they for?"

"Hmm?" He looked up from the infopage he had been reading and glanced over at her, apparently surprised by the question. "What were what for?"

"The samples you asked for. I still can't figure out what you wanted them for."

"Oh." He turned disinterested eyes to look back to his infopage once more, scrolling down to view more of the printed information. "I wanted to add to my collection, that's all."

"Collection? You collect genetic samples?" Strange thing to collect but she had heard of stranger still. She pondered for a moment, trying to reason out why he might collect such a thing but finally gave up. "Why?"

"At first, I was looking for something. Something that was – and remains - very important to me. As my collection grew, I began developing my own research methods for studies on an assortment of other topics and the samples I had already gathered worked very well as a resource for testing and refining those methods.

After I no longer needed the samples themselves, I began generating a database of the data I had collected, which I occasionally use to run analyses or to test for unknown compounds such as the one found in your samples. Now my database contains a collection of almost every life form known to all inhabited planets. This collection has allowed me to continue my search and has occasionally helped others with needs such as yours."

M'Tarl blinked in surprise, not sure how to react to that information. Just how long had he been gathering samples? The list he had given her didn't even come close to the extent he had just described. "What were you looking for?"

"My home."

She blinked for a moment, not sure she understood him correctly. "Your home? Do you not know where that is?"

"I know where it was," he explained, "but it is no longer there. My hope is to find it somewhere else."

She should have expected that his answer

would be as confusing and inscrutable as everything else about the man. How could someone lose their home? Perhaps he meant something different than what she had interpreted his words to mean. Home could mean a great deal of things, after all, so perhaps he was looking for something a bit more mobile than the planet or system of planets that most people considered to be their home. Planets and planetary systems may be known for a wide range of odd and unexpected behaviors but disappearing was not among them.

She considered asking him for more information but then decided against it. At best, she would receive another cryptic answer that initially sounded as though it would answer her question but would ultimately not only fail to answer the original question but also bring about more questions. At worst, she would offend the man. While she was not naturally opposed to offense, she saw no reason to damage their still-developing relationship. Instead, she turned back to the control panel so that they could continue their journey.

"I overheard something about the Tyrannus system a while ago," he changed the subject as she entered the coordinates into the navigation control panel. "A relatively new group moved there recently and has pretty much taken it over. Something called the Iron Gauntlet. Have you heard of them?"

"I have." She activated the autodrive so that as soon as they were a safe distance it would engage. "Are you familiar with a group known as the Deck?" When he agreed that he knew of them, she wasn't surprised. "The Iron Gauntlet used to be part of the Deck but were ousted when their missing leader returned." Once the instructions were set, she settled back into her chair and turned to face him. "Do you think they're the reason this drug is being manufactured there?"

"For the past number of years, the Deck has been manufacturing and selling a chemical that is similar in composition to ZB-2. Many of the manufacturing facilities and distribution centers were shut down and those responsible were apprehended by Triad during the recent change in leadership."

"So you think they fell back to the Tyrannus system because of that?"

He nodded. "I do. If these people were ousted at the return of the Queen of Diamonds, and if they wished to continue their campaign of fear and violence, they would need a place where they already had a foothold, somewhere safe and familiar where they could begin to rebuild their forces. In order to do that, as I am sure you are well aware, many credits would be necessary."

"And if they already knew how to make this drug, that would give them enough credits to build whatever they wanted."

"Indeed." He closed his infopage and tucked it into a pocket before settling back into his seat and closing his eyes. For all appearances, he fell asleep almost immediately.

M'Tarl wondered whether he was actually sleeping or whether he simply wanted to end the conversation. Given how he had communicated with other clones earlier, she suspected he was actually deep in conversation with them and simply didn't want to be interrupted. Turning back to her console, she left him alone.

A rough hand on her shoulder woke her the following day. "We have arrived."

She yawned and blinked, looking around in confusion. Had she fallen asleep at the console again? A large brown planet loomed before them, clearly visible through the forward-facing window. Parts of the planet were covered with a massive, swirling storm mass but other parts appeared tranquil, almost serene in the silence. Barely any water showed on the visible half of the planet, but the console readout showed that there were adequate levels of humidity in the air. Along with the humidity were a handful of other substances, some of which were toxic to most humanoids.

She reached forward and disengaged the autopilot, which had stopped the ship at a safe distance well outside of the atmosphere. Rather than heading for the planet's dangerous surface, she aimed the ship at a small station that orbited the planet, just outside of the highest atmospheric levels.

The station was an early rudimental example of a space station, clearly designed and built for people who hadn't yet mastered the art of space travel. Even worse, it was small at less than half the size of even the small stations to which she was accustomed elsewhere in the galaxy. White and silver panels covered most of the surface area, some designed to deflect the heat from the planet's yellow sun and others designed for easy access when repairs would be needed. Script covered many of the panels, most of which was in a language M'Tarl couldn't read. Massive solar panels stretched out from both sides of the station, angled to capture a portion of the available energy from the nearby star. While it had a handful of docking ports, most of them appeared to have been recent additions and upon docking she discovered that artificial gravity either wasn't a part of the station's design or hadn't been activated.

"I will remain here."

She turned back to look at Jeoh in surprise as she slipped a breathing apparatus across her face. The device helped to filter out the toxins in the air, allowing her to breathe and converse normally. She detested wearing it, as it caused even more of a sense of claustrophobia than anything else, but she detested becoming ill even more. "I figured you'd want to come with me. Where I go, you go, and all that. What happened to change your mind?" She held out an extra breathing apparatus in case he didn't have one.

"No gravity," he explained simply. "It messes with my digestion."

She sighed and tucked the device back into its storage compartment before maneuvering herself into the access port, "Fine. Just don't go anywhere while I'm gone." While the security panel was locked and keyed only to her personal identifier, she wasn't willing to put enough faith in anyone to just believe they wouldn't steal her ship from her. She had made that mistake only once, during her first year of service with the council. Once had been all it took for her to learn and appreciate the need for appropriate levels of caution.

Not that he needed it, she reminded herself, as the man could just appear wherever he wanted without the use of a ship. While she didn't regret her choice of specializing in the mental arts, there were times when she wished she had a little more skill in teleportation and other travel skills.

She maneuvered herself through the entryway, not entirely surprised to see that it led to an old-fashioned umbilical. She was thankful that she was small, as all Qadar were, and wondered how larger species could possibly fit into it. Unless Jeoh could fold himself into a much smaller form or could change forms entirely, he would have had difficulty following her even if he had decided to join her.

Worse, the umbilical looked as though it had seen better days and she eyed it critically, wondering how much longer it would give protection against the freezing temperatures and high levels of radiation beyond. Some places had worn thin, revealing the metallic framework that held it all together. Patches were clearly evident in places, showing that there were areas in which the material had given way completely. It creaked and groaned as she moved, even her own meager weight seeming to strain the aged metal. Given everything she had already seen, all she wanted to do was to get what she needed and get back to her ship. Preferably before the station gave up its fight against the planet and crashed back to its surface. "How is a place like this even still out here?"

When the airlock at the other end of the umbilical opened, M'Tarl was prepared to be equally unimpressed with the station's interior as she had been with its exterior and she wasn't disappointed. Narrow tunnels led from the airlock deeper into the station, with handles placed at regular intervals along the walls. She used these handles to propel herself through the tight opening, where there were only a few feet of clearance between floor and ceiling. Years of training kept her expression neutral, not wanting any action or expression on her part to keep her from getting what she needed and exiting the station successfully. Overhead, or at least in the area she considered to be a ceiling, a fan clicked on as she passed, blowing cold air down her back and sending a chill down her spine.

The temperature inside the station was warmer than the frigid temperature outside, but that wasn't saying much. Had she been planning to spend much more time in the confined space, she would require much warmer clothing and possibly a set of lined gloves to keep from freezing. The only reason her breathing wasn't causing tiny clouds to form around her was due to the apparatus she wore, which caught her exhalation just as it fed her inhalation. Probably a good thing she had worn it, she realized. With no atmospheric controls in the station, obvious by the temperature if for no other reason, there would be nowhere for the moisture to go.

Finally she reached a larger open area in the center of the station. Cables and machinery were bolted to every inch of wall space, including the ones beneath and above her. No more handles were placed against the walls, so she carefully used some of the more stable-looking pieces of metal to maneuver. This chamber was marginally warmer than the umbilical had been, but not by much. Handling the metal in order to guide herself from the entry further into the room was just on the border of painful.

On the opposite side of the chamber, a young-looking Pode leaned comfortably against the wall, appearing to be perfectly at ease in the strange environment. Podes were strange creatures, not ones known to inhabit the Tyrannus system, so seeing one here was unexpected at the very least. It was bulbously shaped, with a smooth head and an assortment of appendages, tentacles or antennae, M'Tarl had never known, dangling beneath. Its singular eye was facing in front of it, watching a panel embedded into the wall upon which danced strange shapes and symbols. This was the closest she had ever been to one of the creatures and although she wasn't scared, she wondered what its presence there could mean. There had to be a reason for it to be there, more than just the distribution of ZB-2, didn't there? The Pode seemed to have either not noticed M'Tarl's arrival or it didn't care.

"How much you need?" it asked as she moved closer. The voice came from the panel the Pode had been watching rather than from the Pode itself.

"Single dose," she replied. Jeoh had said that he only needed a gram or two in order to do his evaluation, so the amount she had requested would be more than enough.

The Pode finally turned toward her, apparently surprised at her answer. "One dose? Kinda long way to come for just a single hit. Sure you don't need more?"

"Yeah, I'm sure." Recognizing that most people likely ordered much larger quantities that were intended for distribution, she explained, "Boss wants a sample before making any large purchases."

Satisfied with her answer, at least to the point that it didn't question further, the Pode reached behind itself with one tentacle and pulled a blue canvas packet from a narrow opening between some of the machines. It opened one end of the packet to reveal sleeve upon sleeve of small white packages. Some of the packages were quite large, more than enough to sit comfortably on M'Tarl's hand, but others were smaller than the buttons on her console. "Fifty credits," it explained as it pulled out one of the small packets.

Despite the information she had been given, she had fully doubted that she would be able to find the promised distributor of ZB-2 inside the archaic station, but she was surprised to discover that the only item sold in that station was the drug she sought. "What about oxygen refills?" she asked. "Food? Water? Fuel?" Even the most rudimentary space station carried at least the most basic of supplies for travelers. For this place to carry none was astounding.

"Nope, none o' that stuff. You want something like those, you need to go to a different station." The Pode held the credit reader out toward her with another tentacle, indicating that the conversation was over. "You want the stuff or not?"

Thoroughly unimpressed, she transferred the required credits. It was likely far more than she needed and cost more than she had wanted to spend but if it gave Jeoh the information he needed in order to restore her psionics, any price was one she was willing to pay. As soon as the transaction was complete, the Pode tucked the canvas back into its hiding spot and returned to its original pose, attention focused on the still-moving screen.

M'Tarl turned around and headed back down the cramped hallway toward the airlock. This was the first time she had been on that station and, if she had her way about things, it would be her last. If the purchase she had made didn't turn out to be the key to returning her psionics, she was going to be sorely upset. Even more than she already was. She squeezed back into the airlock, resisting the temptation to look closely at the wounded material around her. Instead, she took great care to not touch any of it, afraid that even the smallest inconvenience to the material would turn out to be all the excuse it needed to cause a critical failure.

When the airlock on her own ship finally opened, which seemed to take an extraordinarily long time, she pulled herself inside and latched the door, thankful to be alive and to finally be able to rip the uncomfortable breathing apparatus from her face. She sat just on the other side of the door, breathing in clean, healthy air and fighting to calm her nerves, before making her way to the cockpit. It had been a long time since she had been so thankful for the atmospheric controls in her own ship and the steady temperatures inside.

Jeoh, as usual, was seated there, infopage in hand and reading quietly. He finally looked up as she dropped into her seat. "How did it go?"

Rather than answering verbally, she held the small white packet over toward him. "If I never have to go back in there," she explained, "it will be too soon."

He nodded quietly as he accepted the packet and tucked it into a pocket. "I had heard that this is not a comfortable place to visit, one of the reasons I opted to remain here. But this," he patted the pocket where he had just placed the drug, "should be more than enough for our needs."

"Exactly what I wanted to hear." M'Tarl took in another deep, calming breath as she turned to her console. "So where do we go next?"

"I believe the best place for us to go is to my laboratory."

"Your..." she looked over at the man beside her in amazement. "You have a laboratory? As in, an actual lab, somewhere?"

"I do." He looked over at her with one eyebrow raised. "Did I not tell you that I perform a great many experiments? That kind of activity requires a laboratory."

She sighed and closed her eyes. No matter what they were doing, he always managed to find a way to surprise her. Eventually, she supposed, she would get used to it. "Okay. So where is this lab of yours?"

# SHIP DEFENSES

"Approaching target destination, Captain."

"Perfect. Place us into a holding pattern and keep us here."

While the ostensible goal of the Stingray's arrival in the Onoquoi system had been to deliver a shipment of promised supplies to the Qadar, Captain Stump Numperel understood the truth behind their mission, a truth that hadn't been shared with many outside his immediate command. He had recently been promoted as captain of the Stingray, one of the fastest, most maneuverable, most powerful, and heavily armed and armored warships in the Triad fleet, so delivery of supplies was far below its intended design and usual assignment. Many of the crew had balked when they heard what they were being instructed to do but he had overruled them all. After all, it was the captain's job to know what their mission was and to ensure their directives were followed to the man.

The delivery wasn't the only cargo onboard the Stingray. A trio of large machines waited in a separate hold, drop pods loaded and ready to launch them at the planet. These mecha weren't the latest models, nor were they in and of themselves anything fantastic, but they had been designated for display at the planet's annual equipment show regardless. These three mobile armor platforms, as well as the pilots who stood on the grated walkway between them, were actually part of the promised delivery of supplies to Onoquoi.

"You guys ready for this?" Captain Numperel pocketed his comm and looked over at the group of mecha pilots before him. He hadn't ever worked with the Wrecking Crew before, but their reputation preceded them. Enough so that he had come personally to see them off, even though his normal position was on the bridge.

The team leader, a woman designated with the odd code name of Buzzkill, nodded and eyed her teammates in turn. "Everyone understand that we're to be on our best behavior, right?" That last comment was directed specifically at the cyborg on her left, a half-man, half-machine pilot known as Legion.

"I know. No installing other people's tech unless I've paid for it."

The third member of the team giggled at the forlorn expression on Legion's face. "If I didn't know any better," Glitch offered, "I'd think you were disappointed."

"Of course I'm disappointed. The only place that has better tech than down there is on Lovus."

"No upgrades." Buzzkill's voice left no room for argument. She checked her comm and nodded. "Looks like we're at the drop site, so let's get settled in."

The trio separated, each heading for their own mecha. "Think we can get one of these when we get back?" Glitch called over as he climbed up the machine toward the pilot compartment. "Just imagine how much better we could be if we had a ship like this!"

"Don't let Geist hear you say things like that," Buzzkill admonished him as she opened the hatch on her own machine. "He might be tempted to accidentally overshoot the target next time he's putting you into position."

Stump took a few cautious steps back as they all locked into place, ensuring that he remained beyond the barrier and in the safe zone. One by one, the hatches opened, jettisoning the trio out into space, rocketing with guided systems toward the planet.

They weren't freefalling, as the drop pods would slow their descent as they approached the surface, small maneuvering thrusters would ensure that they landed precisely where they needed to be. Once the last of them disappeared, the hatches slowly closed.

As with most warships, the Stingray came with its own contingent of support, both in terms of fighter vehicles and standing troops, making it truly one of the greatest mobile assault platforms in Triad's arsenal. Normally, such a ship would be placed at or near the front lines of a battlefield, perfectly designed to function as a mobile assault and defense platform. Elsewhere, warships such as the Stingray were being used to break advancing forces, to cut through enemy defenses, and for myriad other strategically important maneuvers. For it to be stationed in what should be a quiet and peaceful star system was unusual, to say the least. For it to be tasked with a simple package delivery was even more so. At least the delivery of the Wrecking Crew made it feel like slightly less of a wasted mission, even if they did normally have their own ship bring them to and from their targeted areas.

"Contact the Voivode Council," he pulled

out his comm once again to instruct his communications officer as he headed for the lift back to the bridge. "Let them know that their promised supplies have arrived."

"Understood, Captain."

Stump didn't monitor the communication as it passed from his ship to the waiting council. His men had been stationed with him for months, even years in some cases, and he trusted each of them to do their assigned tasks with both precision and quality. In a pinch, any of his highest-level officers could take over and perform their job with little to no interference from him, and he rewarded their dedication by not monitoring things too closely unless it became absolutely necessary. Micromanaging had never been his thing, before joining Triad and after rising to the officer's ranks within the military. That was the way he had run his unit before he had been assigned captaincy of the warship and it was the way he intended to continue operating.

That didn't mean that he wasn't curious about why the Wrecking Crew had just been deployed to Onoquoi. Their presence on the planet almost made his own warship unnecessary.

"They're sending a contingent to pick up the delivery," the comm officer called over. "Estimated time of arrival is two hours." While technically the Stingray could enter and exit the planet's atmosphere, it was a difficult and slow trip to make due to the size of the ship. Had it been any larger, the very idea would be impossible. Since the need for the necessary supplies was not urgent, the Voivode Council had agreed to send a small group up into space to meet them as the Stingray maintained orbit.

They waited patiently for the contingent to arrive, who came in a small lander. The trio of Qadar looked around in amazement as they stepped out of their tiny vehicle, the reaction was expected. Not many people had gotten so close to a ship like the Stingray and many were excited to see it. Feeling magnanimous and knowing full well what their true orders were, Stump authorized a short tour of the ship, excluding any areas that contained classified equipment.

"This ship is amazing!"

"How old is she? When was she built?"

"How many missions have you been on with this?"

"How many troops does she carry?"

"What kinds of armaments does this ship have?"

"Are there any less restricted versions of this ship that we can get for our military?"

The questions came one after another in typical Qadar rapid-fire succession, clearly demonstrating the visitors' excitement. The crew tried to answer as many questions as they could, deferring many of their answers due to confidentiality agreements, as they came. The tour ended back in the landing bay where they had arrived, where a wooden crate containing the promised supplies waited. The crate was quickly loaded onto the lander and the visitors reluctantly boarded their own ship and headed back to their planet to complete the delivery.

Once the lander was clear of the warship with their crate on board, an unassuming transaction compared with most assignments the crew of the Stingray were normally tasked with, Captain Numperel changed the positioning orders and placed his ship near the border of the Onoquoi system. The distance they traveled from position to position was not great, but the strategic advantage of their new placement was not lost on anyone. Once they arrived, it was only a matter of waiting to see what would happen next.

Forces from both A.T. and the Iron Gauntlet had been closing in on the Onoquoi border the Stingray was now parked in. Stump wasn't sure whether or not advancement from either force would shift with their arrival. Under normal circumstances, their presence would be enough to dissuade any would-be attackers but A.T. had long since proved it had little fear for Triad's might and the Iron Gauntlet was something new, so nobody quite knew what their views on much of anything may be. He scanned the panel in front of him, locating and evaluating each of the threat-marked ships within weapons range, wondering what would happen next. Chess had never been his favorite game, but he knew an invitation to attack when he saw one.

Moreover, he wondered whether the Wrecking Crew was monitoring the same thing he was from their position on the ground. Should he send them the information he had? No, he decided. He needed to trust in them. If anything changed that they couldn't know about, he'd let them know when it was needed.

"Orders, Captain?"

"Hold," he answered without looking up from his screen. "Our objective was only to deliver the supplies; we will hold here until we receive new orders."

"But sir," the weaponmaster objected, "there are quite a few armed ships in this area, most of which do not appear to be friendly." He indicated his display, which confirmed multiple threatening vehicles, the same ones Stump himself had just been monitoring. Even those that weren't already within threat range could quickly move to become a problem with rea-sonable ease.

Stump didn't mind the objection, it was the job of the weaponsmaster to watch out for inbound threats, after all. "I am aware of both the threat and their proximity to our current location. But my orders remain to hold for the time being." He finally looked up at his weaponmaster. "If they fire on us, feel free to defend with all due force. Until that happens, my orders stand. We hold here."

Much as he, along with the majority of his crew, wanted to join the Onoquoi defenses, knowing that they had the ability to com-pletely negate the current threat, his orders were clear. The Stingray, all Triad ships for that matter, was expressly prohibited from actively joining the battle unless specific conditions were met. The most likely of those conditions to happen, given their current position and the potential aggression of the inbound ships, was that they would be attacked. If they were so much as actively targeted by a single craft, he had the authorization to use the full might of the Stingray and all of its resources against those foolish enough to fire upon them.

Even worse for any would-be attackers, the mecha he had just sent planetside weren't un-armed, as most of the other display vehicles likely would be. Those three mecha, with the weaponry and ammunition he had seen and who knew what else had hadn't spotted, were more than sufficient to do an equal amount of damage on their own.

Would anyone take the bait? Only time would tell.

He watched and waited.

# FIVE MILLION CREDIT LIFE

Galeah had been having a very good day. Breakfast had been lovely, wedges of sliced dewmelon and fresh berry and sweetnut muffins shared with her husband Strider before he went off to work. Once he went along his way and the dishes had been cleaned up, Galeah had gone out herself, this time to the local diner to meet with the Gossip. As usual, she'd had a wonderful time, catching up with both those she saw regularly and many she did not. She even had the opportunity to meet a handful of Qadar she hadn't previously encountered, which was always a good day in her opinion. One thing she loved above all others was meeting new people of any race. As always, the Gossip meeting ended just before noontime, which was plenty late in the day for a social call. Particularly when those she intended to call upon were in the group known as Posse.

Posse as a whole were known for their late-night behaviors and troublesome antics. Every bar, nightclub, and street dance braced for impact any weekend where the weather was good and Posse was known to be in town. Many people wondered why Triad kept such childish people among their ranks, certain that it was folly on Commander Moore's part, or perhaps just a softness directed at the team due to the amount of time they had already served. Only those in the upper ranks of Triad knew the truth as to their actual value. While she was no longer among those ranks, Galeah had known from the beginning the true worth of the troublesome team. The fact that Gazer had been one of her best friends for most of her life only cemented that knowledge.

She drove her sleek, powerful sports car out of town, across the bridge and down onto the island, turning up the winding drive and under the gaudy sign announcing her arrival at Posseville. Not for the first time, she wished that Posse lived just a little further away from Midway. Not that she didn't appreciate having the group close, but it would be nice to really be able to open up her engines when she went to visit them. She stopped in front of their house, turned off the car, and stepped out onto the drive, arranging her skirts to ensure they didn't scrape across the ground as she walked before heading up the short flight of stairs that led to their front door.

Given how frequent a visitor she was at their home, either for a professional or a social visit, she didn't bother with the large brass knocker and simply walked inside. Knocking was pointless, as only those who weren't regular visitors to their home did so. As Troll often whined when people knocked, "that means I need to stop what I'm doing to go see who's here. Why can't they just come inside and announce what they want like normal people?"

"Hello!" she called as she stepped into the foyer. "Anybody home?"

"We're in here," a voice called out from the kitchen.

"Is Gazer in there with you?" Galeah called out as she padded lightly across the highly-polished floor.

"Nope, she's still up in her office." Mouse, the single most nondescript human Galeah had ever seen, answered. Mouse's appearance was no accident, as it allowed him to go places where more obvious people would be stopped immediately. He, on the other hand, was utterly forgettable. His height and build were average, his hair a dull and lifeless color that was too dark to be blond and too light to be brown. Even his eyes were a forgettable shade of brown, not quite dark enough to be chocolate nor light enough to be an interesting honey color. His wardrobe was equally bland, a pair of off-the-shelf blue jeans and a plain dun-colored shirt, all worn over well-used sneakers.

"I think she's working on the new brain jack plans," DJ offered. DJ was far more noticeable than his unit leader, from his ring-encased toes that clacked across the floor to his waist-length brown dreadlocks, which had all manner of baubles and bits threaded and woven through them. Next to DJ stood Troll, the least inconspicuous of the bunch. Every strand of hair that grew from his body was a bright, vibrant blue, with eyes to match. Even more conspicuous was the fact that his hair grew vertically, giving him almost two full feet of additional height.

"I see." The new neural interface designs, brain jacks as DJ had called them, were important but Galeah had more important things yet to discuss with her. "Loathe as I may be to interrupt, I fear I must. I shall head up to see her, then."

"Bring this with you, please." Mouse handed her a plate of food. "She hasn't been down to eat yet today." Of all members of Posse, Mouse was easily the most well-mannered. Whether this was a part of his core personality or a part of his efforts to remain unnoticed Galeah had never determined. Whatever his reasons may be, Galeah always appreciated good manners and his were impeccable.

She accepted the plate and headed for the stairs, padding almost silently down the rainbow-dappled hallway on the second floor until she reached Gazer's office. The door was slightly ajar, not surprising as she often left it open a bit for people to check in on her while she was busy. The only time the door was sealed was when she needed to be left uninterrupted. "I've brought your lunch," she explained as she pushed the door open wide enough to pass through.

"Good timing," Gazer grinned at her as she pushed herself away from her keyboard. "I just kicked off the next batch of tests, so I was going to head downstairs in a few minutes anyway."

"No you weren't," Galeah laughed as she handed over the food. "You were just about to get so completely absorbed into something else that you weren't going to come up for air until dinnertime. If even then."

"Guilty as charged," Gazer accepted the plate and sniffed at it, suspicion playing across her features. "Please tell me Troll didn't cook this."

"No, it appeared that Mouse was the head chef today."

"Good. That means it'll be edible." She took a bite and chewed slowly, eyes closed in delight. "Yesterday Troll brought me some soup that I swear had half a bottle of fish sauce in it."

"That sounds truly hideous."

"You think it sounds hideous? You should have tried eating some of it." She scooped another bite into her mouth. "I'm still having nightmares about that stuff and I'm not even asleep. So what brings you by today?"

"This." She set a folded piece of paper onto

the edge of Gazer's desk. "It's a formal back-ground request from Strider."

"Gee, I'm surprised he didn't want to just bring it here himself." Her voice was flat as she spoke, underscoring the truth. It was generally known that Strider was not a fan of Posse, valuable as they may be, as he was far too straight-laced to accept their antics. He had actually been placed in a position of authority over the team for a period of time, which had not gone well for any of them. In Strider's opinion, the team should be able to achieve the same level of results without all of the ridiculous nonsense for which they were known. For a short while, he had actively tried to get the team disbanded, each member slated to head up a new team designed and operated the way Strider wanted them to behave. Rather than simply accepting his plan, Posse had fought back, threatening to quit entirely if they had to continue answering to him. After a lengthy fight in which neither side wanted to give in, Posse was finally moved under a different leader, at which time the squabbling had ended as abruptly as it began.

"Be nice," Galeah admonished. "Even if you guys don't like each other, he's still only one level below Ryan."

"Yeah, well, so is General Li. He has no power here." She blinked, as though remembering who she was talking to. "Not that it includes you, of course. You're always welcome."

The Qadar laughed. "I'm hardly worried. I'm just glad to not be caught in the middle of you two anymore."

"So who does he want the background on?"

"M'Tarl Nox."

Gazer set the plate down and dropped her feet to the floor at her words. "Why does he want to know about M'Tarl?"

"I can't really explain that," Galeah admitted, "he just asked me to give this to you."

"Well, he's in luck, I suppose. I finished the background on her just a few days ago." She looked up to meet her friend's questioning eyes. "What? I knew someone was going to ask about her, I just wasn't sure who it would be. I figured it would be General Li."

"So what have you found? Or are you allowed to tell me?"

Gazer laughed. "We both know that you're probably the least likely person on this planet to repeat any confidential information. But what I found wasn't all that much. M'Tarl Nox has only existed for about forty years."

"Forty years? That's not possible. I've met her, she is definitely much older than forty."

"I know, particularly for a Qadar. She'd be barely even an adult at that age, so I knew there had to be something fishy going on there." While forty years of age would be well into adulthood for a human, Qadar lived much longer and aged much more slowly than did most other races, so they weren't even considered an adult until they turned thirty. This age distinction also allowed them to live for many years longer than did a human, often advancing well into their five hundredth year, if not longer.

Galeah followed Gazer's standard line of

reasoning, their years of friendship giving her added insight to the woman's thought patterns. "You believe she changed her name. While that is not common, it is not unheard-of."

Gazer shook her head. "I thought that might be the case at first too but it's way more than that. You see, if it had just been a simple name change, I would have uncovered that pretty quickly. Happens all the time, actually. Lots of people change their names when they get married to take on the name of their new family. Some just don't like the name they were given by their parents and choose one for themselves. For most people, this happens once, maybe twice, in a lifetime but some people just can't seem to make up their minds on what name they want, so they get a new one every few years or so. Super easy to track."

Since Gazer hadn't mentioned anything as simple as a name change during her initial statements, Galeah had to assume that she had found a dead-end in that line of inquiry. "What do you think caused this information wall, then? Is it just secured behind a firewall you cannot bypass?"

Gazer laughed at the idea. "No such thing as a firewall I can't get through." Her expression sobered. "I think she didn't just change her name. I think she erased her entire identity." She took another bite of her lunch and chewed quietly while Galeah thought.

"Her entire identity? Why would someone do that?"

"I have a couple theories, but I don't want to give anything away prematurely."

"Do you know who she was before that, or is this all the information you have?"

Gazer raised an eyebrow at the idea, her fork hovering in the air. "Oh, come on! You really think I'd drop something like that on you and just leave it be?" She shoved the bite into her mouth with emphasis, as though to accentuate her point.

"Of course not. Your curiosity knows no bounds." She pulled up a chair and had a seat, certain that this would take some time.

"For M'Tarl to have erased her identity,

that means that there had to exist someone previously, someone who disappeared around the time M'Tarl appeared. I went through the records and found quite a few, most of whom I have confirmed actually died."

Galeah looked thoughtful. "Forty years or so ago was during a pretty heavy portion of the war, so there were a lot of casualties at that time."

"Exactly. But I still had to wade through all of them to make sure that her disappearance wasn't just hidden within a standard casualty list."

"Is that where you found her?"

"Nope. All of the casualty lists turned up accurate, everyone reported to be dead is actually dead. However, I did find something else interesting while I was digging."

"Do tell."

Gazer set down her plate and turned to her keyboard to begin clicking. "I believe that before M'Tarl was M'Tarl, she was known as Shahi Barloe. Now, Shahi Barloe was a student at one of the academies on Onoquoi, as are most who are that young, as I'm sure you are already well aware." When Galeah nodded, she continued. "There was an explosion at the academy while she was there. While the damage from the blast wasn't overly extensive, it was determined after a rather extensive investigation to have been caused by sabotage, not by accident as they had originally believed. Three deaths were reported as a result and only one body was found afterwards." She swiveled one of her screens to show the news report of the blast.

"Three people? That sounds like a bit more than a minor explosion." Galeah leaned in closer to peruse the article. "Did they uncover who was responsible for this? And who were the two who weren't located?"

"No culprits have been identified. The academy did a pretty thorough search, no fault there, but they weren't able to uncover much that would lead to an identification. Of course, they had suspects, but I've already ruled all of them out. But that's really beside the point anyway." She took another bite of her lunch.

"As far as the other two victims, one of them was a male, which was obviously not M'Tarl. Pretty sure she's actually a female and not just female-presenting. The other one was a female named Shahi Barloe." She scrolled down on the screen to show a photograph of Shahi Barloe, who Galeah had to admit bore a striking resemblance to M'Tarl Nox.

Noting the look of recognition in Galeah's eyes, Gazer nodded. "I saw that too. Spitting image, right? I looked into Barloe's background a bit. She came from a fairly unsubstantial background. She did, however, show quite a lot of promise in her training in the psionic arts."

"This girl was a psionist?"

"Correct. She specialized in mental stuff, surface scanning and the like, but was woefully lacking in the teleportation training she attempted."

"I thought it was exceptionally rare for people to specialize in more than one kind of psionics."

"That's correct. Apparently, her attempts

were early in her training, before she had settled on the mental path. There's no record of it but if I had to guess, I'd say that her lack of skill in movement-based skills drove her to choose the direction she went. At the time of her disappearance, she was a class two psionist but − and this is just my opinion, mind you − she could have easily advanced another class or maybe even two in the years since her disappearance."

"But that doesn't answer why she disappeared like that," Galeah challenged. "Even if we do accept that this person became M'Tarl Nox, which I see nothing in your information to dispute, what could have driven someone to disappear like that? You yourself said that there wasn't anything in her background that was interesting and if she was still early in her training, she certainly would have wanted to continue. Particularly if she showed promise for advancement, which you seem to believe she had."

"I do. In fact, I'm pretty certain of it. Between the recorded skill level in Barloe's official records and what I know of M'Tarl's skills today, which I don't expect to be complete at all, I'd say she's advanced considerably. Other than the blockage she's dealing with at the moment, but I'm not counting that for this conversation. But all of that is aside from the point, as I also think I've uncovered the reason why all this happened in the first place, why she died and recreated herself into M'Tarl Nox. For one, I don't think that the others were supposed to die, I think that was just a horribly tragic accident. But I am absolutely positive that her death was intentional. Or, at least, her apparent death."

"Do you think someone tried to kill her?" On the surface, it sounded reasonable but nothing in the information she had just been given indicated that anyone would gain by Shahi Barloe's death.

"No." Gazer pulled the monitor back to face her once more and typed a moment on the keyboard. "While the death was determined to be accidental due to the sabotaged equipment, there was a payout made to the families of each of the victims. A pretty substantial one, actually. Each family received five million credits for their loss." As she spoke, the printer behind her whirred to life, spitting page after text-covered page.

"Five million? That's more than most people make in years, quite a few of them. Plenty of people would do worse to get their hands on that kind of windfall. Sounds like a pretty good reason to me."

"That's what I thought at first, too. But then, I uncovered something even more interesting."

"What's that?"

"I don't think Shahi Barloe ever received the money. Nor did M'Tarl Nox. Even though the payout never reached her, I think the money was the entire point of this whole thing. That payment of five million credits is almost precisely the amount her younger sister needed in order to pay for a lifesaving operation. I won't bore you with the details, but it really was a matter of her life for her sister's." The printer quiet once again, she pulled the stack of pages from the catch tray and slipped them neatly into a folder marked Priority.

"You believe that she arranged her own death so that her sister could afford the surgery?"

"It's just too coincidental to think otherwise. The timing of her death and the badly-needed payout just line up a little too well."

"Didn't the original investigators uncover this after the accident?"

Gazer shook her head. "It doesn't look like it. It seems to me that they just wanted to sweep the whole thing under the rug and make it all go away as fast as they could." Given the nature of the explosion and the amount of damage it had done, no academy would want anyone to fear attending, or to fear sending their children to attend, so matters like that were often handled with as little fanfare as possible to keep the general public from ever becoming aware of the hazard.

Galeah was sympathetic to the girl's dilemma. She wondered how many people, if faced with such a choice, would have made the same decision. "Do you think she meant to die? Or do you think she had planned to fake it all along?"

"I really can't tell. Do you want me to keep digging and see what I can find on that?"

"No, that will be fine. Go ahead and continue along with what you've already been working on. This will suffice for now."

"Before you go," Gazer stopped her as she stood to leave, "take these with you." She handed over the file folder.

"What is this?"

"The latest reports on the brain jacks. All of the testing so far is sound, so I would say that they're ready for implantation."

"I thought you said you were still running a batch of tests on them."

"I was. Those completed just a few minutes ago. Everything came up green, so we're good to go."

"Wonderful. As I understand it, the Wrecking Crew have been waiting anxiously to get their hands on these."

"I'm not surprised," Gazer chuckled. "Buzzkill's been overdue for an upgrade for quite a while now." It was because of this demand that the new devices had been required in the first place.

Galeah hadn't been surprised either. Because of the unusual mecha piloted by the team known as the Wrecking Crew, particularly their unit leader Buzzkill, and the strange methods used by their team, they relied heavily on the implanted devices. Most people who witnessed them in action or even just read the reports couldn't imagine how the mecha pilots could get their machines to behave the way they did. The team always said it was because of the neural interface ports implanted in their skulls. "Strider will be quite pleased, both with what you found on M'Tarl and her history but also to know that these are ready to go."

# ASTEROID

M'Tarl flew, following Jeoh's directions, into the asteroid belt near the center of a small, unassuming solar system. As far as her readings indicated, there was no life present on any of the planets around the small, dim sun. The asteroids themselves weren't as thickly-packed as they were in some of the similar belts she had traversed but there were more than enough of them to keep her attention on her controls, not wanting to crash into an un-noticed chunk of rock and ice. The autodrive could react quickly enough to dodge most of them but she needed to maintain a level of awareness to ensure nothing snuck past. Most of the debris were large pieces, easily noticed and avoided, but others were smaller and harder to detect without the assistance of the ship's sensors. Not for the first time, she was thankful for the natural Qadar reaction time, which was widely understood to be faster than the average person.

"It's just up ahead," Jeoh indicated a spot on the display, "not too much further now."

When they arrived at the indicated location, M'Tarl stopped the ship, uncertain as to how they could be in the correct place or if Jeoh had somehow given her incorrect coordinates. They were still in the asteroid belt, as she had expected, but the place he had indicated that they needed to go to was nothing more than a large chunk of asteroid. It was easily the larg-est asteroid in the field, double or even triple the size of the surrounding rocks, almost the size of a moon or a dwarf planet, but there was nothing else to distinguish it from everything around it. "Are you sure?" she asked doubtfully. As far as M'Tarl could tell, it was nothing more impressive than a chunk of rock that had begun forming into a planetoid by absorbing the surrounding materials. There was no way that his laboratory, as he had called it, could be located on such a place.

"I am certain," he responded without looking up at her. "We are at the correct place. Please continue ahead."

She had heard of some large asteroids in other places where the system's residents had placed small science stations on them, both for research and mining purposes, so perhaps his laboratory was something akin to those. Her own rationality sounded false to her, as even from the distance they were at she could clearly see that there was nothing on the asteroid but ice. The asteroid was more than large enough to land on, so she adjusted her trajectory, heading for what appeared to be a safe place to land.

"Do not change course," he objected. "We are not headed for the surface."

"If I don't change course, we'll just crash into the thing. How is that going to help any-body?"

"We will not crash. Just have a little faith."

She lowered her brows and looked at him from the corner of her eyes. "Faith? You've got us headed for a direct impact with the side of this hunk of rock and you want me to have faith that we somehow won't crash into it?"

"That is correct. Just head straight ahead from here."

She had no idea what he was up to or how he expected his instructions to make sense to anyone, let alone her. On one hand, she doubted that he had brought her out here in some sort of a suicide mission in order to get her to crash into the asteroid but, on the other hand, if his stories about being one of many clones were true, suicide may have been his purpose all along. Was his presence with her now just part of a scheme to kill her, a scheme which she had fallen for completely?

She shook the thoughts away. If his intentions had involved her death, there were many more ways to achieve such ends that were far simpler to pull off than this elaborate plan would have to have been. Besides, she strongly doubted that Gazer would have sent her to meet him if she had any suspicion that he would try such a thing. She had spent a little too long, she supposed, surrounded by people who wanted her dead. It had made her suspicious of everything. She continued the course toward the asteroid, slowly, ready to manually override the controls the second she detected a problem.

The asteroid loomed larger and larger in her display screen, quickly taking up the entire field of view. As they advanced, she could see pockmarks where smaller pieces of debris, the same type she had been watching out for only a few moments before, had impacted the frozen rock. Her muscles tensed and her breathing leveled as the ship moved closer and closer, far too close for M'Tarl's comfort.

Just as she was about to override the

controls, certain that they would crash into the asteroid, a hole opened in the side of the rock. A door, camouflaged well enough that even her sensitive sensors and acute vision had been unable to detect, slid open to reveal a landing bay directly in front of her, hidden by the stone-covered facade. M'Tarl let out a low whistle, impressed.

"I had told you," Jeoh snickered next to her, "there is nothing to worry about."

She decided to let the smirk slide for now. "What is this place?" She had seen some hide-outs that were tucked away from view, some deep underground and others tucked away in a forgotten corner of a space station but this was by far the most exotic she had ever seen. Until that moment, she had never even considered the possibility of hollowing out an asteroid and building inside of it. Or was the asteroid in and of itself a fake, stone surface cleverly applied to a more standard frame to blend in with the rest of the asteroid belt?

"It is my home."

They landed just inside the door, which

closed securely behind them. Her ship's external sensors indicated when the cavity had filled with breathable air but M'Tarl was hesitant to leave the safety of her ship. It wasn't that she was unfamiliar with the location, as she spent much of her life in unfamiliar situations and locations. It wasn't that she didn't trust Jeoh, at least as far as she trusted anyone she had only just met. But there was a sense of eeriness about the asteroid, an uncanniness she couldn't quite put her finger on. Had she still had access to her psionics, she likely would have already created a full mental map of the asteroid, including any and all points of escape, but that was just as blocked to her as everything else was. Finally, she realized that she would need to leave the ship and follow him into the mysterious asteroid eventually, so she may as well just get it over with.

"You appear nervous," Jeoh pointed out as she stepped onto the cold metal flooring. "I assure you, there is nothing to worry about here. You are and will remain perfectly safe."

"Forgive me if I don't feel immediately

comfortable stepping out onto an asteroid with no protection," she retorted. "Just give me a moment to adjust, will you?"

The floors and ceiling were not stone but instead metallic sheeting, riveted together to form a solid boundary. None of the rocky exterior was visible once the doors closed, no windows shone to the outside space. Bright lighting illuminated the room from a series of strip lights high overhead, casting strange shadows across the floor in all angles. The room itself was far more than large enough to park her small ship inside, it was easily big enough to house a dozen or more ships that size. Where she had expected the steel underfoot to be slippery from the icy temperatures, she was pleasantly surprised to discover that not only was the temperature in the landing bay comfortably warm, the steel plates across the ground were textured to allow extra traction while walking. She stared around in amazement as she followed him through a small airlock door at the far end of the chamber.

Beyond the door lie more hallways, wider and taller than those in most surface buildings. The textured steel flooring continued down the hall but the walls changed to the more common plastic alloy found on most space vehicles. Soft light filtered into the hall from the ceiling and control panels were set into the walls at regular intervals. None of the panels were illuminated and Jeoh paid them no mind as they walked past.

As they progressed deeper into the asteroid, she began to notice familiar things. What had appeared from the outside to be nothing more than a large asteroid, almost the size of a small moon, was in reality a carefully camouflaged space station. "This is amazing," she said as she stared, wide-eyed at the interior. "Where did you find this thing?"

"I made it," he explained simply. "This piece of rock is the last intact portion of my planet."

She looked over at him sharply, horror and sympathy warring across her features. "Your planet? What happened to it?" He had mentioned something about losing his home once before but she hadn't expected that he had meant the entire planet or that the planet in question had actually been destroyed. She looked around in fresh wonder, realizing just how much this innocuous-looking rock must mean to her strange companion. Was the asteroid belt outside more of the remnants of the same planet?

"I am still trying to find that out myself. I was away when it happened. Upon my return, this piece was the last part I could find."

While M'Tarl had willingly foregone her own planet, no longer considering Onoquoi her home world despite it being where she had spent the formative years of her life, she couldn't imagine what it would be like for the planet itself to disappear. Her greatest sense of reassurance was that, although she left them all behind, the people who had once been important to her were safe in their homes, able to live out their lives peacefully because of her absence. She reached up and traced the outline of the silver ring suspended from her neck, the single memento she had taken with her into her new life, as she considered what that would be like.

"The asteroids outside, are those part of this planet as well?"

"No. My original home was located far away from this place, in an area that has not been well traveled for some time now."

"If it was originally so far away, how did it get from there to here?" While it was possible for debris, even entire planets, to cross the galaxy and move from solar system to solar system, that process took an extraordinary amount of time.

"I added drive and navigation systems so that I can travel where I need to go in order to complete my work. While it looks like a space station, it is actually more of a large ship than anything else."

"You've mentioned your work a few times. What kind of work are you doing?"

"Oh, nothing you need to worry about. A little bit of this, a little bit of that. Mostly just my own research. Here we are."

They entered a large room where ten nude

people, each almost completely identical to the man standing next to her, slept inside a series of vertical tubes attached in a line along one wall. All of the tubes, including the otherwise empty ones, were filled with a yellowish liquid that glowed softly in the dim room and each tube had a monitoring computer attached to the exterior. Life signals and other, less fathomable, statistics displayed in green, orange and red text, none in a language M'Tarl could decipher, across each panel. "Are these more of the clones you mentioned?" She couldn't think of what else they could be, but the question escaped her, nonetheless. Why did he need so many of them?

"They are. This one here," he tapped on the side of one tube, "is the one you initially met with."

"Why is he back in a tube? Aren't those just used for clone generation?" She leaned in closer, curious to confirm with her own eyes that the man she had met was the same as the man in the tube before her. This was the first time she had ever seen a cloning facility in person, and it fascinated her. Question after question whirled through her mind. Was the fluid inside standard biogel, or was he using a compound of his own design? How long could these clones be kept in their tubes? Just how long did it take for him to reproduce?

"Normally they are, that is correct. These are on standby, not needed for anything at the moment. It is easiest to store them when they're not in use, but they can be released at any time they become needed."

"Are there others?"

"Many. The rest are either in long-term storage or are active and working in other areas of the asteroid."

Despite his assurance that the massive complex inside which they stood was a ship, not an asteroid or a station, he still referred to it as an asteroid, a fact she found curious. Before she had the opportunity to ask any further questions, her comm unit signaled an incoming message.

"This is Caro, I'm not sure if you remember

me," the person on the other end explained. "We met at the Gossip not too long ago."

She remembered him, he had been seated at the table next to her. Most of her conversations had been with him and the other people at the table alongside them. What struck her as unusual was the fact that he was calling her. As far as she could recall, she hadn't given anyone at the gathering her contact information. "I remember you. How can I help you?"

On the other end, she could hear the comm unit being passed to another person. That exchange was further evidenced by the different voice who continued to speak with her. "We had thought you were dead," the mysterious voice explained, "but let me tell you how pleased we are to discover you are still alive."

M'Tarl's blood ran cold and all of the color fell from her face. All excitement about discovering more about the cloning process in general and Jeoh's laboratory in specific evaporated in an instant. That voice, she was sure, would haunt her for the remainder of her life, the last voice she had heard before waking up in her own grave. It belonged to the vile creature who had tormented her for weeks before her apparent death and subsequent escape. "Let him go. He has nothing to do with any of this."

Jeoh, noticing the shift in her demeanor, stopped walking and turned to face her fully. She could feel his inquisitive stare but hoped that he wasn't prying into her mind. None of the telltale pressure of intrusion could be felt but a powerful enough psionist could easily hide his activities. He stood still as a statue, waiting to see what would happen.

"We would be happy to let him go," the voice taunted, "on one condition."

"Let me guess," she deadpanned, "you want an exchange." How had he even gotten ahold of Caro? Did these people have access to Lovus? Was Triad somehow involved? No, she shook her head. There was no way they had anything to do with these people at all. There had to be another explanation.

"We knew you were a smart one. You come to meet us, alone, at a location of our choosing.

Bring what we want with you and hand it over like a good girl. Once we have what we want, we will return Caro to you."

"And if I don't?"

"If you decline our generous offer, if you don't show up at the meeting, or if you bring anyone with you, you will still get Caro. One piece at a time."

She had dealt with them enough to know that they meant every word they said. Either she arrived as demanded or Caro would be dead. For a brief moment, she wondered whether they would be as careful in their determination of his death as they had been at her own but she dismissed the idea as pure fantasy. Now that they knew they'd been mistaken with her, they weren't likely to repeat their failure. While she didn't know Caro well personally, she was related to him by more than blood. All Qadar felt the same bond of kinship with each other, so his loss on her hands was unacceptable. "Fine. Where do you want to meet?"

After agreeing to their demands, M'Tarl

ended the call and spent a few minutes in silence, eyes on the floor, brows furled and arms crossed, fingers tapping against elbows. Her mind raced as she tried to come up with a way to save Caro without having to follow through on her promise to his kidnappers. Idea after idea flowed through her head, each one rejected and sent along its way as soon as it arrived. As prepared as she had been for this type of situation in the past, she was woefully unable to come up with a viable solution this time.

Perhaps her brain really had been damaged, as the loss of her psionics shouldn't have had such an impact on her decision-making capabilities.

"Want to tell me what that was about?" Jeoh's voice broke into her rampaging thoughts.

"A friend has been kidnapped," she explained, her voice deliberately much more calm and even than her feelings dictated. While Caro was technically not a friend, she didn't see the point in explaining the precise nature of their relationship. If Jeoh's studies were anywhere near as extensive as he had indicated, he should already know about Qadar kinship. "They want me to meet them so I can get him back."

"I assume this means they want something from you," Jeoh said softly. "What do they want?"

"Something I'm not prepared to hand over. But I need to figure out a way to get Caro out of there without getting myself killed in the process."

"Do you truly expect them to hand him over when you arrive?"

She shook her head. "I am positive that neither of us would make it out of their clutches alive. After all, they've already tried to kill me once. As soon as they get what they're after, they'll do it again. This time, I'm sure they'll do a much more thorough job of it."

"Are these the same people who did this to you?" He tapped the side of his own head, apparently understanding without needing to be told that she did not want physical contact at that moment.

She nodded. "So he's already dead, whether I show up or not."

"Is this Caro important to you in some way?"

"Not especially. I've only met him the once."

"Then don't go." Maybe he hadn't been as aware of Qadar relationships as she had thought.

"I considered that," she admitted. "Normally, something like that wouldn't be enough to draw me out, but there's a catch."

"What's that?"

"If taking Caro doesn't work, they'll just grab someone else. They'll keep going until I give in and give them what they want." Even though she had no particular connection to most of the people who could be in danger, she was not comfortable being the cause of so many deaths. Those who had already died because of her, either by design or accident, continued to weigh on her. Most of the time, she was able to keep the thoughts at bay but at times like this, they all came back to haunt her.

"What is it that they want you to bring with them?"

"Something I cannot give them." Her voice was colder steel than the encasing the landing bay. "They can kill me but they can't have what they want."

"Is this worth your life?" he asked, one eyebrow raised.

"It is worth so much more than that. My life would be a small price to pay to keep what I have secure. My death would be but one among millions, billions, trillions even, if they get what they want."

"Then it sounds like we need a plan."

She nodded. "And we need one fast. Otherwise, my only real option to stop widespread death is to show up without what they want, both of us die, and they no longer have any way of getting their hands on what they're looking for." After another long moment of thought, she headed back in the direction she had come.

"Where are you going?"

"My ship," she explained. "I'm going to

meet with them." The kidnappers hadn't given her much time, likely correctly assuming she would attempt to thwart their plans. In only two steps, Jeoh caught up to her and walked at her pace back down the long metallic corridor.

The flight to the meeting place took a short amount of time, during which M'Tarl and Jeoh spent talking, hashing out ideas and attempting to come up with a plan that would save both her and Caro. Most of Jeoh's plans, unfortunately, involved his presence alongside her. "I have to go alone," she explained yet again. "They were very clear on that."

Jeoh had been loath to let her go on her own, despite her insistence. However, he recognized that she was serious about her intentions of meeting the demands placed upon her, with one exception. It was her life, therefore her choice. "I understand your point of view but I have a suggestion that, while not exactly legal, would allow you to survive the encounter. With just a little bit of luck, Caro should survive as well. Are you willing to hear me explain this idea?"

As he explained his plan, M'Tarl nodded thoughtfully. It was every bit as crazy of an idea as she had suspected it would be, bordering on illegal but she didn't have time to consider the reaching impact of this decision. There were definitely holes in his plan, places where failure could be the result, but it was the best option she had so far, not only to save her own life but that of Caro as well. Finally, she agreed. "That just might work." If it turned out to land on the opposite side of legal, she would deal with the ramifications of her decision later. "How long will you need to get this set up?"

"Not long at all. Please stay here for about twenty minutes."

As he disappeared, she glanced down at her console. The meeting was scheduled for only a few minutes after his expected return, so if anything went wrong in the meantime there would be very little time to adjust. She didn't like having to rely on such constrained plans but it was the only option she had left. Other than the obvious, at least.

M'Tarl arrived on planet only a minute before the expected time. Her tormentors, Caro in tow, were already in place waiting for her. "We are pleased to see that you arrived alone," one of them called out to her once she was within speaking distance. "Glad to see that you are willing to follow our instructions. Now give us the rest of what we want."

"That's not going to happen," she responded. "We've already been over all this. You've killed me once already, so you should know I'm not just going to hand anything over to you."

One of the men pulled out a handgun and leveled it at Caro's head. The weapon was archaic, nowhere near as powerful as ones available elsewhere in the galaxy but still more than enough to end a life. Particularly when fired at point-blank-range. "Last chance," he called over. "Hand it over or your friend dies."

Praying that Jeoh's plan would work as well as he believed it would, she shook her head. "You can kill us both," she offered, "but you will never get what you've been after. It's mine to guard and all my information about it will die with me." Her last hope was that because they had failed to extract the information previously using psionics, they wouldn't attempt to do the same again this time. She wasn't nearly as well defended now as she once was.

"As you wish." Even as he spoke, the report echoed across the clearing and a fine red mist sprayed out, spattering across her face and clothing. The air was instantly filled with the scent of copper as Caro's lifeless body slumped to the ground. M'Tarl squeezed her eyes closed, knowing but not wanting to see what would come next. Gunshots hurt, as she knew from plenty of first-hand experience. She just hoped they didn't drag it out again like they did the last time. A quick death would be a blessing.

"Give us the codes." His voice had turned much colder and more serious. "You know we'll kill you. Isn't your life worth anything?"

Nails digging into palms, she took a deep breath and tried to calm her racing heartbeat. "No matter what I do," she opened her eyes and looked squarely at them, "you're going to kill me anyway. Even if I gave you the codes, which I'm not going to do, I'm dead already. So you might as well just get it over and done with already."

"As you wish." She watched as his finger squeezed the trigger, releasing a small flash and a cloud of gunpowder. She had just enough time to notice the report as it echoed through the clearing before feeling the first bullet impact, then the second.

With the third, the world went dark.

# BLOCKADED PLANS

---

The leader of the Iron Gauntlet was having a bad day. Truth be told, Bryck had been having a lengthy series of bad days, an endless stream of them, enough so that it was starting to feel normal. Considering further, he was beginning to have difficulty remembering how long it had been since he had experienced a day he would think of as being a good day. So many of his plans, plans upon which he had been heavily reliant in order to see his ultimate goals come to fruition, had fallen through, despite the extensive planning he had personally seen to for each of them. The latest setback involved the unexpected arrival of a Triad warship on the edge of the Onoquoi system, effectively blocking his troops from entry.

Worse, this was an event that he had been personally assured would not happen. Despite all the assurances, however, there it was. Taunting him and daring him to make a move. An entire section of the Onoquoi border was effectively blockaded by the presence of a single heavily-armed warship.

The intended start to the takeover of the Onoquoi system had been absolutely deflected by that ship, a fact that soured in his stomach. A single warship was bad enough but this was no ordinary warship. This was a hammerhead-classed ship, the least likely type for him to be able to overcome. And where there was one Triad ship, many more were waiting just out of sensor rage but willing to move at a moment's notice. The heavily-implied warning that the ship silently carried with it was clear. Any move forward against the Qadar would be considered an act of aggression against Triad as well.

The Iron Gauntlet was nowhere near strong enough or equipped well enough to handle that kind of a threat. His only hope of overcoming Triad's show of force would be to partner with A.T., a partnership that hadn't yet come to fruition. A.T. was the only military in the galaxy that had proven strong enough to stand toe-to-toe against Triad. Unfortunately for Bryck and the Iron Gauntlet, the size and power of A.T. had resulted in his inability to open communication with them, as nobody seemed willing to speak with the newcomers. He had reached out to every contact within the group he had been able to uncover, to no avail. So far, all of his attempts to communicate with the powerful force had been rebuffed.

He didn't like being rebuffed.

A.T. weren't his only options. There were still a few contacts in his list who may be able to assist with his current and most pressing problem. He pulled out his portable comm and made a call.

"You said that Triad would not get involved with the Onoquoi takeover," he said without bothering to introduce himself. If the person on the other end of the comm wasn't already aware of who he was and why he was calling, there was a much larger problem at hand. "You assured me that they wouldn't be a problem here."

"They aren't," his contact answered. "The Voivode Council was explicitly prohibited from contacting Triad in this matter and Triad was told to stand down. Your expansion should meet little resistance."

"If that is the case, then would you mind explaining to me why one of Triad's warships is parked directly in my path?" His voice rose as he spoke until he was almost screaming into the comm.

"They what?" Surprise registered across the comm. "I... I was unaware that there were Triad ships of any kind in that quadrant at all. I had been assured that they had all been pulled away."

"Oh, they were. We watched as every one of the Triad ships in the area cleared out. That's what we'd been waiting for so that we could start our move. But now, just as we're getting ready to go, they parked the Stingray in full view. It's like they're taunting us, daring us to try and get past them."

"The Stingray? That's ship's supposed to be..." his words faded as pages rustled, indicating his search for information. "It's supposed to be in port for resupply right now."

"Well, unless its resupplying with Qadar supplies, that's definitely not where it's at." He pinched the bridge of his nose. If the Interplanetary Government couldn't even keep track of Triad, how was he supposed to rely on any of the information that came from them about anything else? They were beginning to be as useful to his cause as the Deck had been when he left it. What other information had he gotten from them that was wrong? "Get it out of there," he demanded. "I don't care how you do it, just make it gone."

"I will see to it immediately." There was a lengthy pause. "About that other matter…"

"Which matter would that be?" Bryck growled again. He had to resist the urge to throw the comm against the closest wall at those simple words. The only reason he didn't give in to his original impulse was due to years of restraint from doing precisely the same to the former King of Clubs, a man who had deserved far more than just to be thrown against a wall. But the King was no longer his concern, as he had bigger matters to focus on now. Despite his feigned ignorance, he knew precisely what the man was asking for. The 'other matter' his contact had referenced was the cornerstone of their working relationship. Not a conversation could be had without this or similar inquiry. Personally, he was tired of even thinking about it, let alone discussing it.

"The codes for the Qadar weapons array. Last I heard, you had a good opportunity to get those for us."

"Oh, yes. The weapons array. Well, we've hit a bit of a snag on that," Bryck admitted.

"Another snag? Those seem to be accumulating lately. What happened this time?"

"Initial reports show that our source didn't survive the interrogation." He had been furious when he received the news that M'Tarl Nox had been killed, as he had been depending on the information within her head. Worse, she had been buried in a shallow grave near the interrogation site, a grave that had later shown to be vacant. How his people had mistaken a living Qadar for a dead one was beyond him. He had personally seen to the punishment that had been meted out for that blunder.

"So where does that leave us? Are there any other sources for this information?"

For a moment, Bryck considered letting his contact continue under the belief that Nox was dead but ultimately decided against it. If he needed their assistance to deal with her in the future, he didn't want to have to explain why he had misled them. "We believe there may be," he said finally. "Actually, it's the initial source." He picked up a report from his desk and eyed it thoughtfully.

"You're not making any sense." Confusion practically radiated from the comm unit at the words. "You just said the source was dead, now you're saying you can still get the information from her."

"That's the thing. We had initially believed her to be dead but recent information indicates that she was revived. Possibly a clone or some similar method was used, we still aren't sure how. I have men looking into it but they're hitting dead end after dead end. We intend to go back after her soon and use, shall we say different, tactics to get what you need from her as soon as she is located again."

"Make sure that you do. We need those codes and we need them as soon as possible." Those codes were the reason the Iron Gauntlet had initiated its assault on the Onoquoi system to begin with. Once they had those codes in hand, the entire Qadar government would fall almost immediately and without argument, particularly if Triad continued to be held at bay. If they didn't manage to get the codes, they would have to take the weapons array by force. The presence of the Stingray posed a big obstacle to that contingency.

"In the meantime," he responded, "get that warship out of my way. The last thing I need right now, the last thing either of us needs, is to get tangled up with Triad." Worse, if Triad figured out what they were up to, they would likely move in a much larger force to stop them, orders or no orders. Their commander was obnoxiously decisive like that.

When the Ace of Spades had begun negotiations with the Interplanetary Government, back while he had still been a ranking member of the Deck, he had allowed them to believe that he was willing to hand over the codes in question once the weapons array was under his control. Now with the ever-growing Iron Gauntlet behind him, Bryck was becoming less and less excited with the idea of the Interplanetary Government getting their hands on the weapon. Most of his efforts of late had been involved in keeping the agency from uncovering what he was truly planning, which was much larger in scope than ever seen in the history of the galaxy. The first step in achieving that plan was getting the weapons array under his control, a step that was almost within his grasp. As far as he was aware, his contact remained clueless as to his actual intentions, which most definitely did not include handing over the keys to the most powerful weapon in the galaxy. Small blessings could be found even under trying circumstances, he supposed. At least this was something going in his favor.

Either way, the weapons array would be under his control soon, of that he was certain. The men he had sent out to retrieve the codes were under very explicit instructions to come back with what he wanted. He wasn't interested in any excuses about them falling for more of M'Tarl Nox's tricks. Other than that, he just needed the Interplanetary Government to keep Triad from meddling in his business until he got what he needed.

He was hardly in the mood to deal with any more surprises.

# ARRAY OF LIES

---

"You and I both know," Galeah explained as she settled into one of the plush leather seats, "that I know a lot more about Qadar history than anyone else in Triad."

"And a good afternoon to you as well." Ryan Moore set aside the paperwork he had been perusing, curious to see why Galeah had made a surprise visit. As welcome as she always was in his office, for informal visits she normally preferred that they meet at the little tea shop down the street. For her to have invited herself into his office meant that she had something more important than a social call on her mind. "And yes, I know that fact quite well."

"I remember the devastation during the galactic war."

"I would expect no less. You were there for most of it."

"Correct. I also recall the day I found out exactly how devastating our most powerful weapons truly were." She shuddered at the memory. "And I recall the chaos that happened when an entire solar system was annihilated with those same weapons."

Ryan's brows furrowed and he leaned forward in his seat. There was no chance whatsoever that this was anything as simple and casual as a social call and the nature of her musings bothered him. "I remember reading about that in my Qadar History studies at the academy. I don't recall which solar system it was that got destroyed, though."

"Their name doesn't matter. Well, to be

certain, it matters greatly, but not in the context of this conversation."

Ryan had to admit defeat. He had no idea where this conversation was supposed to be going or what was expected of him. It had been a long time since he had seen the normally unflappable Galeah flustered. "You've confused me."

"I know, and for that I apologize. But all will make sense soon." She took a deep breath and straightened her back, as though trying to gather the courage to speak of whatever was truly on her mind. She brushed her hands across her skirt, plucking at a piece of invisible lint.

As she settled herself, Ryan pressed the button on his desk to notify his assistant to hold his calls and then waited patiently for her to finish gathering her thoughts. There had only been a few times in recent history where Galeah had felt the need to talk with him in an official capacity without notifying him ahead of time as to the topic and these situations almost never turned out well. Any news she had to impart was likely to be game-changing, either for Ryan himself or for Triad as a whole. Or both, depending on how he managed the situation.

"They were supposed to have been a threat, you see. Never to be used in actuality."

"The antimatter arsenal? Yes, I recall having heard something along those lines." That weapon had been the most powerful weapon the Qadar – or any other race in the galaxy, for that matter - had ever created. "I also heard something about claims that it didn't work the way it was expected and that's why it was used."

"Correct. At first, our announcement that we had the weapon was enough to keep all threats at bay, but that didn't last for long. Despite our continued assurances that we had a functional weapons system, those who had their sights set on us began to believe it was nothing more than bluster."

"Because you hadn't used it, they didn't see the threat."

"That's exactly right. Everyone believed it

to be a bluff and some decided to call us on it. To see if the weapon truly was as ready and as effective as our claims indicated. After many years of harassment and threats, the Voivode Council gave in to the pressure. They decided that it was time to prove ourselves, to show that the weapon was every bit as devastating as we had claimed it to be. To this end, they ordered us to fire it on one of our neighboring systems."

Ryan knew the story, although he was loathe to interrupt. The small amount of antimatter fired at their sun had caused it to explode, similarly to a supernova, annihilating in an instant all of the planets that had circled closest to the star. The initial blast had caused a chain reaction as the rest of the system's planets exploded fantastically and there were no longer even remnants to show that the star or its planets had ever existed in the first place. Barely even a debris field had remained where a sun and a small handful of planets had once resided. Rather than explaining his understanding of the situation, he waited for Galeah to continue.

"Once it was used, when we discovered the horrifying effects of the weapon, the council decided it was too dangerous to ever use again. They ordered the entire array destroyed." She plucked at the seam of her skirt, as though trying to remove an invisible loose thread. "We knew it would be devastating but we had no idea just how widespread the damage would be. That was why we had chosen to fire at the sun, everyone had assumed that it would be able to absorb the majority of the explosion."

"All of this was a long time ago," Ryan spoke gently, "and those weapons have been gone for a long time. There aren't even any people researching how to build new ones, as everyone agrees they're simply too dangerous. What are you so concerned about?" For as long as he had known the elder Qadar, he had never seen her in such a state of agitation. "Is someone looking into them again?"

"No, I don't think so. Or perhaps yes. Or perhaps I don't quite know right now. I just knew that you needed to be informed, as quickly as possible."

"Informed of what, exactly?" He pushed a cup of tea, one of her own blends that she had gifted to him on his last birthday, in front of her. "I can't do anything if I don't know what's going on." The tea was more than a simple matter of courtesy, it was made of a blend of soothing herbs that calmed him when he drank it. Hopefully it would work on her as well.

"I know, and I apologize. But I am getting to that." She took a sip of the tea, which seemed to calm her a little. "You understand, of course, that this is highly classified information. I'm not supposed to tell anyone, including you, about it. I must therefore insist that none of this conversation leaves this room."

That got him to sit back in surprise. Normally, he was the one cautioning other people to not repeat what he told them about. He wasn't used to it being the other way around. "The Voivode Council?" he asked. They were the only ones he could think of that could have given Galeah such an order. Other than himself, of course.

They sat in silence as he activated the enhanced security protocols, dropping a series of shutters across the windows that lined his office and sealing the room from any sort of eavesdropping. Once the lights on his control panel indicated the room was secure, he motioned for her to continue.

She nodded and took another sip of her tea and a deep breath. "The official story is that the antimatter arsenal was destroyed but that is not the complete truth of the matter. It took months for us to discover that destroying the weapons wasn't going to be as easy as we thought it would be. The antimatter, which had been created specifically for these weapons, could not be eliminated without devastating effects."

The premise behind the weapon was both simple and devastating. Antimatter, small amounts of material with the opposite charge as normal material, was perfectly safe when stored in a specially-designed chamber, one that the Voivode Council had spent many years and billions of credits designing how to create. The storage chamber was of particular necessity for when antimatter came into contact with normal matter, no matter how small the particles were, both were eliminated from existence as though the positively and negatively charged particles canceled each other out entirely.

"We never found a way to destroy them," Galeah continued. "So we settled on the next-best option."

"What was the next-best option you decided on?" Ryan was becoming even more unsettled by the course of the conversation. While knowledge about the existence and destruction of the Qadar antimatter array was limited but available, the idea that the array still existed had never even been whispered. Even the amount of time he had spent as Commander of Triad had never given him the barest hint of such information. Perhaps he should have made himself a cup of tea at the same time he had made one for Galeah. At the very least, he was certain he would need his antacids by the end of this conversation.

"We locked them away, hidden so deeply that they could never again be found, never again be used. Three individuals, those who knew the truth of the matter, were entrusted with the location and access codes to the weapons. Everything about their continued existence was erased, buried under lies and false stories of their safe dismantling."

This was quickly growing much worse than he had anticipated. Ryan fixed himself a cup of the tea, certain he needed something to loosen the knot that was quickly building in his stomach. The tea wouldn't be enough, he decided, so he pulled a bottle of antacids out of his desk. Hopefully the lightly sweetened tea would cover the taste of both the chalky medication and the news he was hearing.

"If what you're telling me is true," he said finally, "and these weapons are still out there somewhere, we need to ensure their safety and security. This isn't just about the Qadar and the Voivode Council, not just about Triad. This could potentially impact the entire galaxy." He settled the bottle onto a corner of his desk and took another sip before asking, "What happened to those three people you mentioned?"

"I am one of them. You and I both know that the secret I hold is secure. The second set of codes was given to a man who died soon thereafter, without passing along the information to another, so his information has also been secured."

"And you're sure of this?" When she nodded, he asked, "What about the third?"

"The third person passed his knowledge to his daughter before dying." She carefully set a folder on his desk and slid it over in front of him. "She, in turn, passed the knowledge down to one of her two children. One of her daughters was reported to have died in an explosion at the psionic academy where she was training, approximately forty years ago. While that young lady had a sister, we confirmed quite some time ago that she did not gain the family secret. In fact, she almost died herself many years ago but the settlement for her sister's death availed enough credits to save her life."

"This would indicate that you are the last to know about the existence of these weapons and how to activate them." Visible relief spread across his face as he accepted the folder. "That's good to hear. So we just need you to tell us where these weapons are so we can arrange security for them."

The relief was quickly replaced with anxiety as Galeah shook her head. "You and I both know I cannot reveal that, not to you or to anyone else. However, the information is not secure."

"Why not? You just said you were the last to have this information, so how could anyone else know about it?" If everyone else who had known the secret was dead and Galeah hadn't told anyone, what could that possibly leave?

"This report came from Gazer." She tapped the folder once again to bring Ryan's attention to it. "I recently discovered that the girl who died in the fire is rather less dead than we had been led to believe. Living under a new identity, she has already been captured and interrogated once. She refused to divulge the information they were trying to extract but her psionic abilities were destroyed in the process. While she was believed to have been killed yet again as a result of that activity, she yet lives."

"How many lives does this woman have?" Ryan asked, more to himself than to her. "I assume the loss of her abilities has something to do with the information they were trying to extract." He could see where the logic was headed and he didn't like it one bit. He opened the bottle of antacids with one hand while holding the file with another. The way things were progressing, he was certain to develop another ulcer.

"She was last registered as a class two psionist but even that has fallen into question. Gazer also agrees that she could easily be a class three or even four by now. That is assuming that she continued her training after her supposed death." She smiled with little humor. "At least, her first supposed death."

"Let me guess," Ryan finished chewing the tablets and looked up from the pages in the folder. "Her psionics were specialized to mental focus?"

"Correct. We expect that her abilities were the reason she was able to hold the secret for so long. Now that those have been damaged, there are no safeguards in place. If she has no means by which to protect both herself and the secret she holds, even a rudimentary psionic scan will uncover the truth."

Ryan flipped through pages in silence, scanning each of them quicky and reading others more carefully. All of the information Galeah had just explained was clearly written out in the pages, over half of which he could identify as having come directly from Gazer, giving him no reason to doubt a single word. He now understood exactly why Galeah had come unexpectedly into his office that morning and why she had appeared so harried. Confirmation that the Qadar antimatter weapons array continued to exist despite the official reports of its destruction was bad enough.

That information paled in the knowledge that someone out there held not only the precise location of where the weapons could be found but also the activation codes to arm and use them. This put not only Triad but all of the systems in the galaxy at risk.

"You mentioned that she has already been interrogated to gain this information. Can we confirm that this is the information that was sought?"

"She has refused to divulge what information was desired from her interrogators but there is plenty or reason to assume this to be the case."

"Do we know who these interrogators were?"

"We do," Galeah admitted, "but you're not going to like it."

He sighed and pinched the bridge of his nose. "I already don't like any of this."

"It was members of the Iron Gauntlet."

Ryan was already stuck between a rock and a hard place. He had sidestepped direct orders to not interfere with the Qadar system by sending one of his most powerful warships on a fabricated supply delivery. That maneuver had already resulted in two days' worth of angry communication from the Interplanetary Government, insisting that he stand down. As much of a hassle as that maneuver had turned out to be, at that very moment Ryan couldn't be more pleased that he had not obeyed the orders. What he had initially believed to be nothing more than supporting a long-standing ally against invasion had turned out to be much more important than anyone had realized. "I wonder if the Interplanetary Government would let us move to their defense if they knew about this," he mused quietly.

"You cannot tell them," Galeah reminded him. "I told you this confidentially because I know you can hold the secret. But as I said at the very beginning, this needs to go no further than you."

For all of his planning, for all of his contingencies, this was not something Ryan was prepared for. He had never considered that the weapons array could still exist. Nobody knew it hadn't been destroyed other than the three people about whom he had just been informed. Suddenly, he realized that wasn't quite true. "That has to be what they're after!"

"Come again?"

"The Iron Gauntlet has been advancing on the Onoquoi system for some time now. I've moved a ship there to help with the defense, but there was never any indication of why they were moving on the system. If everything you've told me is true, which I have no reason to doubt, that makes it pretty obvious, doesn't it?"

"What are you going to do?" Concern lined her voice in soft velvet.

"I don't know," he admitted. "But I need to come up with something, and I need a plan quickly." He considered requesting permission to act from the Interplanetary Government, but he knew it would be futile. They were already unhappy that he had a single warship in that area, there was no way they would allow him to move more troops in that direction. At this point, it was probably a good thing that nobody was aware that he had a mecha team on planet as well. Without being able to spell out the threat, he would sound foolish even making the request. But he had to do something.

Galeah left as quietly as she had entered but Ryan didn't signal for Coffee to allow calls again quite yet. He had a lot of thinking to do, and he needed no interruptions while he did so.

If Triad didn't do something, those weapons would surely be unleashed. Eventually, he would lose the fight against the Interplanetary Government, and he would be forced to pull the Stingray back. Even if that didn't happen, the Iron Gauntlet would certainly find a way around his defenses and find the weapons array. Once they had their hands on that, all they needed was the access codes hidden in M'Tarl Nox's head. Without the ability to block her mind from psionic invasion, M'Tarl would not be able to keep the information she held a secret for much longer.

If that happened, they were all dead. It was

almost inevitable at this point, and he needed to find a way to stop it.

His eyes slid from the bottle of antacids to a playing card that had been tucked beneath a stack of papers to be reviewed later. He picked up the card and turned it over in his hand thoughtfully, revealing the Queen of Diamonds on the other side. "If anyone can sneak in and find this thing before they do," he mused to himself, "it's you." He turned the card over again a few times as he considered. He wasn't sure how far his trust of the woman went, despite his own personal feelings about her. He respected her, certainly, and he appreciated her aversion to violence, but could he really trust her with something this monumental?

He set the card back down. His eyes moved from the card to the file Galeah had left with him. As he considered what few options he had available, he knew his decision was already made.

He just hoped he didn't regret it.

# DEAD AGAIN

Jeoh, his face a tight mask of concentration, looked down at the limp form of Caro sprawled on the grass at his feet. "As I said," he explained, "this will work."

"And I cannot explain how pleased I am to hear that," M'Tarl said as she helped Caro climb to his feet. "Can we get out of here now?"

"Wait a second," Caro interjected, obviously

still disoriented from the exchange. "Can someone explain to me what is going on?"

"Certainly," Jeoh said, "but not here. We need to be a bit further away just in case they discover the ruse." The world around them disappeared, replaced with a different set of scenery. Where tall grasses and low hills had been was now covered by a dense forest of trees, branches stretching high into the sky above. It was colder here as well, fogging their breath with every exhale. The change was so drastic that M'Tarl briefly wondered whether they were still on the same planet. "I hope you don't mind us teleporting here," he explained once everyone arrived safely.

"Not at all," she replied. "I would have suggested the same myself." She also would have suggested somewhere warmer, as none of them were clothed adequately for the sudden change to colder temperatures but now was hardly the time to complain.

"First of all, we're glad to see you're okay," she explained to Caro. "It doesn't look like they've treated you too badly, so that's a relief."

Panic slowly subsided from his expression, washed away by waves of relief as he realized he was safe. "No, I was adequately treated. They had mentioned something shortly after taking me about not wanting to do too much damage, in case that made you less cooperative." He smiled wanly. "I suppose they didn't have to worry about that too much after all."

"Not in the slightest. Nothing they could have done would have made me less cooperative as I never planned on cooperating in the first place. I never had any intention of giving them what they wanted." She smiled ruefully. "They could have taken Galeah herself and I still wouldn't have handed anything over to them." She chuckled at the idea. "Although, it would have been interesting to watch them backpedal as the entire might of Triad descended on them."

Relief changed to confusion. "Why would Triad show up? Wasn't she retired?"

"Sure, but they tend to take care of their own, retired or not. Anyway, this is Jeoh," she introduced.

Caro stared at the man, slack-jawed. "Jeoh? As in *the* Jeoh?"

"One and the same," Jeoh spoke up before she could answer. "I'm pleased to see that you're safe as well."

He opened and closed his mouth a few times, forming question after silent question before squeezing his eyes shut and shaking his head slightly. "I know that I got shot back there, at least once. How are we both alive?" Caro turned back to M'Tarl. "Not that I don't appreciate it, of course, but I really expected to be dead right now."

"I switched you with a clone," Jeoh explained. "As soon as you were in sight."

"A clone? Aren't those illegal?" He looked back and forth between the pair, doubt evident on his face.

"Not for me."

"It's a good thing he did, too," M'Tarl explained. "They shot you pretty much right off the bat. Had he waited to assess the situation, there wouldn't have been any time to switch you out. You'd be dead right now."

Caro's eyes widened and he looked over at her in amazement. "Did he switch you for a clone too?"

"Yes," she nodded, "I was switched out much earlier than you were. The real me wasn't ever there to begin with. The M'Tarl that you saw back there hadn't actually known anything to disclose or have taken from her, so it was perfectly safe. I'm just glad that Jeoh had a couple of spares he didn't mind losing."

"I see." Caro looked between his rescuers thoughtfully. "So even if they had used psionics to scan you when you didn't give them what they wanted, they still wouldn't have found anything useful at all."

"Correct. It was the safest option we could come up with to get you out of there safely without putting ourselves into direct risk."

"I see." Caro pulled a weapon out of his pocket, a pistol similar to those used by the hostage-takers. "In that case, I am going to need you to stay right where you are."

"What are you doing?" M'Tarl looked at him in amazement. His weapon was similar to the ones that had just been used against him, or rather his clone, which made her pause. Where had he gotten that? The last thing she would have expected was for him to side with the bad guys. Didn't he understand the point of being rescued? She scanned his expression, which showed no sense of camaraderie, no sense of compassion, no emotion at all. Had it not been for his race so clearly displayed across his features, she never would have recognized him as a fellow Qadar by the amount of familiarity in his eyes.

Even as she wondered, she realized the truth. Caro had never been on her side to begin with. He had been a mole and she had been duped.

No, she shook her head, the more likely explanation was that the Caro standing before her, weapon in hand, wasn't the same Caro she had met on Lovus. If that was the case, it would certainly explain why he wasn't responding like a Qadar.

"I assume this isn't your friend after all." Jeoh didn't appear to be disturbed by the turn of events in the slightest. "I had suspected this may happen."

"You knew?" Incredulous, M'Tarl turned toward him, ignoring the weapon for the moment. "Why didn't you tell me?"

Jeoh shrugged. "This was the man who you were so determined to save, so I expected that was your desire. But it seems that his appearance has been altered in order to give you the impression that he is your expected friend." He turned to look at her directly. "I'm surprised you didn't notice, considering how easily you spotted the difference in me."

With his other hand, the imposter pulled out a comm unit. "I'm not dead," he explained irritably to the people on the other end. "And I don't particularly appreciate being killed like that, it wasn't part of the plan." He listened for a moment. "I am with M'Tarl and Jeoh. Yes, I said Jeoh. That seems to be how she's been evading us. Apparently, we were both swapped with clones and teleported to safety. You should be able to get our coordinates off of my comm."

"You're not leaving," he tucked the comm unit into a pocket and turned to face M'Tarl fully, "until you give us the information."

"Not going to happen," she said quietly. "I already told you guys that you can kill me, but I still won't hand it over. Not to you, not to anyone." Considering the quantity of times these people had already killed her, she wondered why they still seemed confused on her willingness to cooperate. The only way they would get the information they wanted so badly would be to rip it out of her head. On the one hand, she was a bit surprised that they hadn't already tried such a tactic but on the other, the fake Caro's comments a moment ago indicated that they were at least thinking about it.

"Then perhaps your friend will have more of a survival instinct than you have." He turned the gun to point at Jeoh. "You're pretty famous for getting into people's heads. Go in there and get me the codes."

"I cannot do that."

"Nobody's leaving until I get what I came

for. Either you give it to me or you both die right here. You willing to die for your friend?"

"We have a contract. I am not allowed to enter her head without permission. She has already clearly stated that I am never to do that."

"A contract?" The imposter blinked in confusion between the pair. "What do you mean, a contract? Isn't your life worth more than hers?"

"Of course not," Jeoh answered. "And if you truly knew even a fraction as much about me as you claim to, you would already have known that."

"In that case," the fake Caro smiled cruelly, "I guess I'll just have to kill you both. After all, we can always find other ways of getting what we need."

"That may prove a bit more difficult than you had expected." Another Jeoh, this one comprised mostly of cybernetic parts, stepped into view, appearing out of thin air directly behind the impersonator. He was joined by two more similar Jeohs, each of which appeared identical to the latest arrival.

"I believe the three of you can manage things from this point," the Jeoh still standing next to M'Tarl said to the new trio. "Do you mind if I teleport us out of here?"

"You're not going anywhere!" the fake Caro shouted. "None of you. Where did these come from?" He stepped closer to the man standing next to M'Tarl, gun still stretched out before him in a threatening manner. "Why are there more than one of you? You're not going anywhere until you tell me what's going on."

"What is going on," Jeoh answered calmly, "is that you have made a series of critical mistakes. I suggest you take some time to reflect upon the decisions you have made thus far. Perhaps, by doing so, you can see the errors you have made, the erroneous assumptions you accepted as fact, and come to a much different conclusion and therefore a different plan of attack from that which you obviously settled upon." The creepy smile played across his face once more as he spoke.

Without a further word or any outward indication, the world shifted once again. This time, Jeoh and M'Tarl arrived at the edge of a small lake, its crystalline surface like glass. A handful of golden-crested ducks glided peacefully across the water, paying no attention to the change in audience. Not even a ripple announced their arrival.

Next to Jeoh, half an arm, gun still clenched in its fist, fell to the ground. "It would appear I missed slightly," he said. He bent over to pick up the discarded arm. "No matter. I'm sure he would have lost this soon enough anyway."

"Are you sure we're safe here?" M'Tarl's mind was still whirling with everything that had just happened. "I assume you teleported those clones to assist us?"

"I did. As soon as I realized that you hadn't been aware of the imposter, I called back to my laboratory. Those three were the first that woke, so they were the ones I brought to our aid."

"What about the real Caro? Is he okay?"

"Most likely. I expect he remains on Lovus

where you last spoke with him. However, that is easy enough to verify."

Even as he spoke, M'Tarl pulled out her portable comm. So long as she was still within range of her ship, the device could link up to it, allowing her to call much further than she would have been able to otherwise. She entered the contact information for Posseville.

"We're sorry," a recorded message at the other end of the comm said, "Posse is not available to take your call at this time. Please leave a message after the tone. If this is important, please contact General Li. If this is Strider, please use official channels to contact us."

Rather than leaving a message that she knew from experience would never be reviewed, M'Tarl swore softly and ended the call. Hopefully they were just sleeping in late or were unavailable for similar reasons. If they were out on a mission, it could take some time before their return. As her only direct contact on Lovus, there was little else she could do to confirm Caro's safety until she either spoke to Posse or returned to the planet herself.

As she pocketed the comm, she looked at the severed arm in Jeoh's hands. The firearm had already been removed, likely tucked away in one of the many hidden pockets or directly teleported back to his laboratory, she didn't particularly care which. "What are you going to do with that?"

"Research."

# HOUSE ARREST

---

Shortly after arriving back at M'Tarl's ship, her communication panel lit up. A call was inbound but the source was restricted. Uncertain as to who could be calling her, particularly from a restricted line, she responded hesitantly. On the one hand, she hoped it might be the Voivode Council, calling to offer her job back but on the other she knew that was unlikely at best. At least, not until she regained the use of her psionics. Another thought she considered had been that the group targeting her was continuing its harassment, a concern that evaporated as soon as she heard DJ's reassuring voice.

"Heya, M'Tarl. You guys still doing okay?"

"Yeah, we're doing fine. Ran into a few snags, but nothing to worry too much about. How are things with you?" Pleased as she was to hear from him, she highly doubted that it was a social call. Despite her earlier attempts to reach him, or any member of Posse, she waited patiently to see what he was calling her about. The fact that he had called from a restricted line wasn't lost on her.

"We're on our way to meet up with you. Where are you located, currently?"

"Currently?" She glanced down at her control panel. "About to leave system so I can engage the compression drive."

"Where are you headed to?"

The nature of his questions, as innocuous as they appeared, gave her a bit of pause. "Why do you ask?" The last thing she wanted was to discover it hadn't been DJ on the other end of the comm, but had instead been yet another imposter. Being fooled once in a day was more than enough for her tastes. Had she already regained her powers, this wouldn't have been an issue as she would have simply connected to Posse directly to confirm their identities. Having to rely on electronic communication was far more of a pain than what she had previously realized. There was simply no easy way to prove who was on the other end of the comm.

"We've been given a new assignment that requires we link up with you guys. But I've got a lock on you, so we'll meet you back at Jeoh's rock."

The call ended and M'Tarl looked over at her passenger. "Did you tell them we were headed back to your place?"

He nodded. "Gazer asked me directly, so I confirmed it. Should I not have?"

"That's okay. So long as you're certain it was her you were speaking with." She sighed and rolled her shoulders. "I suppose I'm still a little edgy from that last meeting." At least one of them was still able to confirm identity. She just wished it was her.

"I had a feeling. You had a strange look on your face while you were talking with him, so I checked with her, just to be sure."

"Thanks." She wasn't sure why, but she was relieved that he'd had the foresight to confirm her suspicions. "Did she say why they're coming to meet with us?"

"She did not."

M'Tarl silently lifted a hand to trace the outline of the ring hanging from her neck as she thought. DJ hadn't exactly been forthcoming with details about the assignment they had been given and how it related to her and Jeoh. "Is this a common thing for them?" she asked finally.

"It happens on occasion," he admitted, "although normally due to the belief that I have broken or otherwise circumvented a law somewhere."

"Do you believe that is why they're coming now? Because of what just happened?" If that was the case, it was easily the fastest response time she'd ever heard of.

"I couldn't say. While technically I broke the agreement by teleporting you without permission, it was done to save your life. I also don't know whether the damage done to the one called Caro was a violation or not. Technically, I am restricted from violating any local laws, but that action was done in your defense, for which I believe there is an exception in the legal definitions. Nor do I know whether I was prohibited from summoning additional clones to our defense. As thorough as your writ of permission was, it did not cover how many of me could be on the planet with you. At that moment, I assumed that meant there were no limitations."

"I can't imagine any of those things would get you in trouble." She looked at him askance. He was taking a little bit of leeway with the writ she had given him but so far everything he had done had been within the bounds of acceptability. And he was correct, she hadn't placed any sort of limitations on how many of his clones could accompany her. To be fair, however, she hadn't realized he was a clone at all when she had generated the permission. Had there been any indication of that, she likely would have included it. "Speaking of your restrictions, I've been curious about them for some time now. What caused you to be under such heavy restrictions to begin with?"

"I've broken my fair share of laws," he admitted. "Mostly many years ago, long before your time. That was what got me locked away in the first place."

"Can you tell me about it?"

He shrugged with one shoulder. "Not a lot to tell, really. As I told you before, my planet was destroyed while I was away, many years ago. When I returned and discovered that everything I knew was gone, I went a little crazy. My wife, my children, my friends, everything and everyone I knew had disappeared in the blink of an eye. I was determined to uncover who had caused such damage, how it had been done, and to hold those responsible for what had been done."

"I had figured on most of that, but it still doesn't explain what caused your incarceration. Unless you acted on something you shouldn't have." She hadn't known about the wife and family part, but it made sense. Not many people enjoyed a life of solitude.

"I did well more than act on something. Are you familiar with the Wytrax?"

She thought for a long moment. "I don't think I've heard that word. What is it?"

"Not a what, it was a who. The Wytrax were a race of people who my planet was in fairly constant conflict with back then. They inhabited a planet in a system next to mine, so we fought all the time, primarily over resources and the like. There was a large resource of materials between our two systems which we had both laid claim to. Looking back on it now, there was plenty for each of us to have more than enough but we both wanted sole rights to it, fearing it would somehow run out before we were able to find more. As of when I left my world, we had recently pushed the Wytrax back and assumed full control of the resource field. They, in turn, were displeased with us and had promised to retaliate. When I discovered the destruction of my planet, I believed the Wytrax to be responsible. That this had been what they meant when they threatened retaliation."

A sinking feeling began in the pit of her stomach. "Tell me you didn't." His story, so similar to those she had heard for most of her life, rang true in her ears. While most races fought on occasion for territory or other resources, few ever took it to the extreme.

He nodded. "I am the reason you've never heard of the Wytrax. They no longer exist because of me."

It was no wonder the man was so feared across the galaxy, even if most people didn't understand why he was so dangerous. Part of her wanted to ask what he had done to eliminate the Wytrax but a much larger part of her didn't want to know. She wasn't sure she was ready to hear about that level of destruction from her companion. She had never heard any of what he had just explained but had no reason to doubt him.

"Originally, I was supposed to have been put to death after my arrest, as punishment for what I had done. I fully admitted to everything, feeling justified in my actions still. More than that, I was comfortable with that decision, ready to die. I felt that, at the very least, I would once again be with my family in the next life."

"But that didn't happen."

"No. Since I am the sole survivor of my race, it was determined that to put me to death would be to eradicate an entire species. Instead, I was locked away and have remained there ever since." His face, still expressionless, somehow hardened at the words.

She couldn't even imagine what it must have felt like. What seemed on the surface to be a rational and magnanimous decision, keeping his species from dying out completely, was in fact the opposite. He was the last of his race, the last of his kind, and without another there would never be more. His life of solitude was far more comprehensive than she had re-alized. To be locked away, the last of his kind, sounded more like an extended torture than a kindness.

"How were you able to make all the clones if you were locked away?"

"I had already made some of them. Seventeen of my original arrests were not the primary me but my clones instead."

"Was that why you had cloned yourself so much? Because your people were gone?"

He shook his head. "My original plan was to locate some remnant genetic samples of my home world and its people so that I could resurrect them. In order to do that, I needed the ability to travel further and investigate multiple locations simultaneously. Cloning was the most reasonable method by which I could do so."

His intense need to collect genetic samples made much more sense at the admission. Having left her own home world and family behind, she could understand his loneliness on some level. Their situations were vastly different, however. She still had her home world, little as it felt like one, and she still had connections with her race, her people, when she wanted them. The depths of his despair had to be far greater than anything she was capable of imagining.

"How did you…"

He interrupted her before she could complete the question. "If you don't mind, I would much rather not discuss this further now. Perhaps later I will be more inclined to answer the remainder of your questions."

They flew the rest of the way in silence, her mulling over what he had disclosed and him watching out the windows in apparent disinterest. Much as she wanted to ask more questions, she didn't believe that prying was in either of their best interests. He was correct; there would be plenty of time to talk more later. When the landing bay doors opened in front of them, she spotted a second, much larger ship waiting for their arrival.

"I see they made good time."

As far as M'Tarl could tell, Jeoh was entirely

unbothered by their previous conversation. But then, she really wouldn't know one way or the other. He never showed any true emotional response to anything and she was beginning to wonder whether he possessed any emotions at all. Perhaps his original race had been somewhat emotionless, she considered. She dismissed the possibility almost immediately, as the amount of rage required to destroy an entire race of people would have been simply impossible for someone who had no emotions. Instead, she wondered whether his clones simply had no emotional attachment to his original crime and the events that had led up to it, a potentiality that she considered likely. If she had been in his position, she wouldn't want her clones to be so buried in grief and regrets that they would be unable to perform their functions either. They calmly walked into the complex, where they found Posse already assembled in the main meeting area. "Hey guys."

"Hey yourself." Mouse stood and approached. As with the rest of his team, he wore the black combat uniform with red badging, which clearly indicated that they were on official Triad business and definitely not a social call. "We've been sent here to meet up with you guys to ensure your safety." He made eye contact with M'Tarl. "Your safety in particular."

"My safety?" She was confused. "Is this about what happened with Caro?"

"Who is Caro?" While M'Tarl explained what had happened with Caro, Mouse signaled over to Gazer, who pulled out her comm. "No, this isn't about that, but thanks for letting us know. We'll check and see whether the original Caro is secure and deal with whatever happens."

"I don't understand."

Having the entire Posse unit in full battle gear standing in front of her was intimidating. Although she had developed a relationship with some of the members of the team, she hadn't previously met all of them. As an assembled group, they were known to be one of the most dangerous in all of Triad. Not just because of the psionic abilities possessed by

Mouse and Gazer, nor by the firepower clearly displayed on each of their gear harnesses. They were dangerous because they were only called in on the most urgent of situations, ones where lives – often many of them – were at stake. Posse specialized in infiltration and espionage but they were more than capable of cutting swathes through enemy troops, should the need arise. In short, they were just like M'Tarl herself aspired to become, an aspiration that could only be achieved by a few additional lifetimes to train and allowing Jeoh to clone her a few times. "Why do I suddenly need extra protection?"

"It's about the loss of your abilities," Gazer stepped forward to explain. "While we already knew that they had been taken, we didn't realize until very recently exactly how much danger that put everyone into."

"How is having you guys here going to help with that?" M'Tarl looked around the group in confusion. "Jeoh's already working as hard as he can to restore them and you said you weren't able to do much beyond this to help on that. Are you going to just travel with me until my powers are restored?" She could hardly imagine a team as powerful as Posse being assigned something as simple as bodyguard duty.

Gazer laughed. "Heck, no. That sounds super boring. No, we're here so I can lift some restrictions on this guy." She pointed to Jeoh as she finished speaking.

"Lift restrictions? I don't understand." M'Tarl didn't like being confused about things and it seemed like she had been nothing but confused and bewildered since her abilities had been blocked. Everyone around her seemed to know a lot more about her situation than she herself did, something she did not find comfortable in the slightest. "Can we take a step back and explain what's going on? I still feel like I'm missing something."

"Sure," Mouse agreed. "But would you mind if we did so elsewhere? I'd really rather we not stay here, if it's all the same."

"I don't think it is all the same, actually. We're here so that Jeoh can synthesize a cure from a drug we found so that he can restore my abilities. Since you all seem to be so concerned as well, I'd rather just do all of this here."

"It's okay," Gazer said as she switched off her comm. "I'm familiar with Jeoh's lab, so I can help him with what he needs to do. As far as Caro, I just confirmed with Galeah that he's fine and had no idea he had been killed. Twice, it seems."

"That's a relief." Much as she had hoped the impersonation had been fully based on lies, she had still held out to the small fear that perhaps the original Caro had been taken and used as a model for the person they had encountered. Knowing that the true Caro was safe on Lovus lifted a weight from her that she hadn't realized she'd been carrying until it was gone.

While Gazer and Jeoh headed deeper into the complex to begin working on the cure, Mouse explained their understanding of the situation to M'Tarl. "First of all, you probably already understand that Jeoh is under some pretty tight restrictions."

M'Tarl agreed. "He told me about what happened with his planet and what he did to the Wytrax."

If Mouse was surprised to hear that, he gave no indication. "Those restrictions cover much more than just where he is allowed to travel, they also restrict his access to advanced biological research and development techniques, as well as anything that can be considered invasive."

"That travel restriction is why he needed the writ of permission to travel with me." She had already assumed as much, as it was the only reason she had come up with for why he had requested it in the first place. "Why does he have restrictions on his access to research techniques? Isn't that what he does?"

"His restrictions have to do with invasive techniques, things that could prove harmful or even fatal to the subject. He's only allowed to perform those types of research on non-sentient creatures. We maintain a list of what creatures he's allowed to experiment on and which he isn't."

"What about his clones? Are they considered sentient creatures?"

"No. Those are on the approved list because despite all appearances, almost none of them are actually sentient."

"So there really is just one mind controlling all of them?" When Mouse agreed, she pressed, "is that the primary Jeoh, the one that's locked away?"

"That is beside the point and something I'm sure you will get the chance to discuss more in depth with him later. For now, I just need to make sure you understand where the boundaries of his restrictions lie so I can explain what our purpose for being here entails."

"I think I've got it, or at least the gist of it. Go ahead."

"Only a handful of people are permitted to lift those restrictions, which only happens under extremely rare conditions. Gazer is one of those people."

"You'd mentioned something to that effect

as well." She looked around at the group. "If he is supposed to be under such heavy restrictions, I don't see why my situation suddenly calls for them to be lifted. That's the part that isn't making much sense."

"We know about the explosion at the academy."

M'Tarl looked from Mouse to the rest of the gathered Posse members, recognizing finally why they were there. For the briefest moment, she considered defaulting to denial but knew immediately that it would be futile. If absolutely nothing else, Mouse could simply rip the truth directly from her brain, should he choose. Unlike Jeoh, he had no restrictions that prohibited his entry into her mind. "How much do you know?"

She listened as Mouse explained about their understanding in regards to her history, from her time at the academy until her reported death. "I didn't cause the sabotage," she explained when he reached that point of the story. "I knew about it and used it as a cover for my own disappearance but I wasn't actually responsible for it."

"We were wondering about that. You know you weren't the only person who died there."

She nodded. "Not at first, I didn't. I learned about them shortly after the blast. Even now, I'm not sure why they were there, as that area of the building was supposed to have been completely closed off to prevent something like that from happening. By the time I heard about them, there wasn't exactly much I could do to mitigate it."

She didn't need anyone to tell her that they knew about the secret hidden within her mind, a secret so dangerous she had been willing to die to keep safe. She wasn't sure how they had discovered what she knew and that she was the one who knew it but there was no longer any point in arguing. With that knowledge, their presence on Jeoh's asteroid made perfect sense. She had been correct, they were only called in when lives were at stake.

Until her powers were restored or she was

dead, those lives included everyone in the galaxy.

"You had more training after you disappeared, didn't you?" Troll stepped forward. "Gazer mentioned that she was positive you're higher than a class two."

M'Tarl sighed and nodded. "I think right now I'm the equivalent of a class four. At least, I was before my powers were blocked."

"Where'd you get the training?"

"The Voivode Council arranged it for me after I joined." She didn't need to explain that she had already been recruited by the council at that point and would have been required to disappear at some point. It was widely known that no member of the Voivode Council maintained their original identity once they joined their ranks.

# BRAIN MATTER

---

"I have something for you." Jeoh stepped into view as he spoke, holding a large vial in his hand. He had spent the past few hours in silence, not even vocally communicating among the dozen or so clones who had been working at the banks of machinery in his lab. M'Tarl had watched them as they worked for a small period of time but had given up on comprehending much of anything. The clones switched with each other so often that keeping track of which was working on what had been the first thing she'd lost track of. Most of the machines and other equipment in Jeoh's lab were ones she didn't recognize and she had no clue what they did. Both of these things, particularly when combined with the lack of verbal communication, made it impossible to understand what they were doing and what was working or not working. She couldn't even tell whether any of the procedures he used were giving promising results. Finally, she had given up on any pretense of monitoring the situation and went back out to the meeting area to wait.

"What's that?" M'Tarl looked up from the news article she had been scanning. It strongly indicated that treaty talks were in the works between A.T. and Triad, which made her curious. None of the information she had received had indicated that A.T. was interested in joining such talks. It was commonly understood that Triad was almost always willing to discuss an end to fighting as they appeared to be far more interested in peace than in war, despite war being their primary function. A.T., on the other hand, was widely known to be resistant to such discussions unless they were backed into a corner and losing the battle. Since that wasn't the case, it didn't make much sense for A.T. to be even considering a treaty with Triad. There had to be an ulterior motive for their change of heart.

She eyed the vial in Jeoh's hand suspiciously. It held a light brown colored liquid which appeared similar in consistency to the unfortunate and yet all too common results of a late night spent drinking.

"I was able to break down the sample of ZB-2. Using that analysis, I have come up with a possible solution for your problem."

"Is that what you're holding?"

"No, of course not. The pieces of the sample are too small now, they've all been broken down so they're microscopic. This is just a nutrient mixture I am testing." As if to accentuate the point, he took a sip from the vial and grimaced. "It could probably use some flavor enhancement." He stoppered the vial and tucked it into one of his pockets before looking back over at her. "I already tested the solution on some tissues I made from your genetic sample and they appear to be reacting well."

"Tissues made from my..." her voice trailed off as her eyes widened at the man. "You cloned me?" While she had agreed to let him modify one of his clones to mimic her appearance, she had understood that to be a singular occurrence. At no time had she given him permission to create a full copy of her and she wasn't entirely pleased to hear he'd done it. Not that cloning her had been expressly forbidden, however. Gazer's warning about his habit of exploiting loopholes rang clearly in her memory.

"Not exactly. Well, yes, but not in your entirety. I only cloned a small portion of your tissues to ensure the solution would work correctly and have no, erm, adverse side effects." He even had the nerve to look sheepish at the admission, or as close to sheepish as he could come.

The more time she spent around Jeoh, or any of his clones, the more she had begun to recognize why the man was so feared throughout the galaxy. It wasn't that he was overly dangerous in and of himself, despite what he had done after the destruction of his planet. Instead, he was dangerous because the sheer concept of what was right and wrong simply didn't appear to be a part of his thought process. He was easily the least morality-driven being she had ever encountered and she had met a large quantity of morally-ambiguous people throughout her career. When presented with a dilemma of any breadth, no matter how large or small it may be, he simply chose the solution that appeared the most rational to him at that time. The entire concept of right and wrong never seemed to occur to him so those ideals were never part of the consideration. "Why did you clone my tissues?"

"I needed to see what effects the sample would have on you and to see how it impacted your system. I did not believe you would be interested on testing against your person directly, so the disposable tissues became a necessity in order to apply and confirm the effects of the compound. Using that, I was able to reverse the process in the clone, erm, tissue, and I believe I have made the procedure safe enough that it can now be used on you."

His words did little to reassure her that she hadn't been cloned. However, she wasn't sure that this was the best time to pick that particular fight. If he had come up with a cure, regardless of the methods he had used, it was worth it. She could deal with any spare copies of herself after her abilities were restored, one battle at a time was the best way to handle the current situation. Despite his admission about cloning her, his overall message gave her hope "So when can I take this cure you've come up with?"

"There are a couple things of which you need to be aware before you do," he explained. "First and foremost, it will not be comfortable to administer."

"Comfortable how?" She wasn't sure she liked where this conversation was going. Every turn they took led her further into darkening territory.

"Well, I suppose comfortable isn't quite the correct word. What I had intended to say was that this will be an extraordinarily painful process. How high is your pain tolerance?"

"My pain tolerance?" She looked at him, slack-jawed. "Why is it going to hurt so much? Isn't it just a pill, or one of your concoctions, or something like that I need to swallow?"

"It is one of my concoctions, that is correct. But swallowing? No. It needs to be administered directly to the source of the problem."

"Source of the problem. I assume that means my brain?"

Jeoh nodded as he withdrew the vial from his pocket once more and took another swallow. "Specifically, it needs to be injected into the portions of your brain that control your psionic abilities. Since you had a recent brain scan, that helped to narrow down the field of focus considerably and will save us much time.”

M'Tarl shook her head. “There's absolutely no chance that I'm letting you poke around in my brain, physically or psionically. There has to be another way.”

“If there is another way,” he explained, his voice far gentler than she was used to hearing from the strange man, “I do not know what it may be. But this has the highest chance of successfully returning your abilities. Not just returning them, but restoring them to their previous levels. It will be as though none of this ever happened.”

“I just need to let you cut open my head. What kind of a fool do you take me for?”

“We agree,” Mouse stepped forward to join the conversation. “The risk of you doing brain surgery on her is far too dangerous. You and I both know that she could die if we let her do this.”

“You also know,” Jeoh turned to face him, “that she will die if she does not get this treatment. At least with this treatment, she has a better chance of avoiding or surviving any further encounters with her friends back there. It is only a matter of time before they catch up with her again and eventually they will succeed. Furthermore, whatever information she has been safeguarding in that head of hers will be in danger as well without her abilities to protect her. Unless I have missed something, that is the very reason you are here right now. I have done everything I can to render this process as safe as possible while still achieving the desired results. It is, in so many words, her best option of survival and your best option of completing your current assignment."

Mouse sighed, unable to counter the argument. "We should take her to Midway General. If she's going to undergo this procedure, she should have medical personnel on standby in case something goes wrong."

"That's not possible," Gazer joined the small group before Jeoh could object. "We all know he isn't allowed anywhere near Lovus. While I can release some of his restrictions, that's not one I have the power to do. And," she raised a hand to forestall any further objections, "he has the skill to pull this off and enough clones to have more than adequate emergency care in a worst-case scenario."

"Additionally," Jeoh spoke up, "I have a better-equipped facility here than what you have down in your hospital. I also have as much or more knowledge than your best neurosurgeons and far more experience."

"That's true enough," Mouse reluctantly agreed. "But if we do it here, then we should at least have a specialist come up to supervise. I don't want the risk of anything going wrong and having to face the fallout of us not having a licensed doctor in the house."

As Gazer turned to make the request, M'Tarl spoke up. "Don't I get a say in all of this? I haven't agreed to anything yet." If someone was going to be poking around in her head, she should have the final word on who was to be doing it and whether or not it was going to happen at all. Instead, everyone was acting as though her agreement to the procedure was a foregone conclusion.

"Of course you have," Jeoh pointed out. "Otherwise you wouldn't be here with us in the first place. After all, we have a contract, do we not?"

M'Tarl watched him walk away and then looked over to where Mouse and Gazer stood at a comm, calling for a neurospecialist from Midway General to be brought to the asteroid ship. How had she gotten dragged into this procedure, particularly when she still wasn't sure what would be done during it? Despite her resistance, she had to admit that Jeoh was correct. Because of her not having her abilities, she wouldn't last long. The Iron Gauntlet would catch up with her, probably sooner than later, and finish the task of killing her. Worse, they may bring a psionist with them and forcibly remove the information she'd been so far unwilling to divulge. He was also correct in his assertion that if she didn't want to get her abilities back, she wouldn't have stayed for nearly as long as she had and she certainly wouldn't still be standing there. Had the need for some sort of experimental procedure not been as pressing as it was, she would have long since returned to her ship and left to find other means of solving her problem.

She just hoped this concoction, whatever it was, would do the job. She wasn't eager to discover exactly how painful the process would be, but she had no illusions that it would be moderate. Despite all of the medical procedures she had received over the course of her life, brain surgery was not one of them. Much as she tried to hide it, the idea scared her. And not just a little. The fact that Jeoh had even bothered to mention the pain levels in the first place practically guaranteed that it would be the most agonizing thing she had ever experienced.

"Doctor Aditi will be available in a few hours," Gazer turned back to where M'Tarl still stood. "He's good, he often works on us when we get messed up in the field, so you'll be taken well care of."

"I know. He's treated me a few times, too." It was somewhat of a relief knowing that her own doctor would be overseeing her treatment, even if he wasn't going to be in a hands-on capacity. Just having him there was reassuring. Even so, she still hoped she wasn't making a massive mistake with agreeing to Jeoh's plan. If there was another route to explore, she would be happy to look into alternative methods, but none so far had presented itself to her and she was completely out of bright ideas.

"It's not too late to back out," Mouse added, apparently reading her misgivings. "Say the word and we'll have you right back out of here and on your way."

M'Tarl sighed. "Where would I go? Jeoh's right and if you guys have done as much research on me as it seems you have, you guys know as well as I do that until my abilities are returned, nowhere will be safe for me."

As though she was expecting such an answer, Gazer nodded her head. "In that case, let's get you prepped so we can get going as soon as Dr. Aditi gets here."

# COUNTING THE BIRDS

"Well, that was interesting," The Queen of Diamonds said as she ended the comm. She stretched out one leg to poke the man lying on the floor with a toe. "You asleep down there?"

"Nope." Knave rolled over, showing her the puzzle cube that he had finished solving. "These things are actually pretty simple once you know the trick." He sat up and stretched, reaching for his forgotten cup of tea on the coffee table. "What's interesting?"

"You remember the Aces who broke away from the Deck when we took back Cardiss, yes?"

Knave scowled. "How could I forget?" He had been highly irritated for almost a month after taking back their base, his dream of exacting revenge for what the Aces had done in his and Diamond's absence thwarted by the cards' disappearance. Even the amusement of sending a gift basket to the FBI, this one with a toy submarine and a 'thank you for your donation' card, along with their signature pair of playing cards, hadn't dulled his irritation. As with many of the other members of the Deck who had shifted loyalty in his and Diamond's absence, almost all of the Aces had disappeared. The pair had spent a bit of time searching for them, their efforts in that arena less than the massive amount of effort it had taken to simply get the Deck back up and running smoothly once again after their hostile takeover. "Have we found them?"

"Not quite yet. But we do have some new information about them."

His interest piqued; Knave turned to face her more fully. Knave was a Tet, a very large race of humanoids who were most easily distinguished by their muscle mass and the third eye in their foreheads. His companion, on the other hand, was part Emovete, a much smaller race with only two eyes, although they were much larger in diameter than all three of his own combined. "Okay. What did we find out?"

"They've re-formed into their own group, and they call themselves the Iron Gauntlet."

"Iron Gauntlet?" He rolled the words around in his brain, not liking how they felt on the tongue. "Sounds pretentious, like they're trying to sound like the new tough guys on the block."

Diamond laughed. "I thought so too. Apparently, they don't have much imagination." She reached forward to take a drink of her own tea. "But the information we just got is that they seem to be focused on the Onoquoi system lately for some reason."

"Onoquoi? What could they possibly want with the Qadar?"

She shrugged. "The information I got was kinda vague, so I don't have all the details. But it seems to me like it's worth checking out."

Neither of them had to voice the fact that they had both been seeking an amount of payback for the people now calling themselves the Iron Gauntlet. While Diamond and Knave had been stranded and unable to communicate with the Deck, a handful of their members had overthrown the group and turned a normally peaceful organization into a horrifying and terror-inducing visage of what it had originally been. It had taken almost a year after their return before Diamond and Knave had regained control of their operation and the losses they had suffered in doing so continued to wound Diamond.

One of the biggest and most painful of those losses, outside the deaths of some of their people, had been the Cardiss base. She had personally chosen that base as a stronghold against all invaders and the Aces had used that fact to their advantage. Cardiss had been the final holdout against Diamond's retaking control of the Deck, and she had been forced to use a new and exceptionally devastating weapon against people who had once been her own in order to do so. While they still technically maintained control of the Cardiss base, it had become too well-known, too closely monitored by many other agencies and groups, not the least of which was Triad, for her to feel comfortable there. Less than a month after seizing control, they had left a skeleton crew in place to maintain the image that it was still fully operational. The rest of the Deck had abandoned the base.

Thankfully, during the time when Diamond was scheming to regain control, she had set up a series of secondary bases. Each of these had been intended to be temporary but they had become much longer-duration locations than she had ever expected. She and Knave traveled among those places on a weekly basis, checking in via comm meetings with the people in each of them practically daily, but none of them were where they spent most of their time. They stayed relatively close to Terros, the only place where they truly felt both comfortable and safe. It had been one of their last remaining safe houses during their absence, one that had thankfully remained undisturbed and was waiting for them upon their return. Because of that, they knew that nobody had uncovered their location when they went home to rest and regroup.

"We have a decent working relationship with the Qadar," she said finally. "And they're closely allied with Triad. While we don't have a great relationship with Triad as a whole, we've been working on building that for a little while now."

None of this was news to Knave, so he waited patiently while Diamond verbally sorted out her thoughts. When her mind was made up and she wasn't willing to listen to alternative points of view, she kept her thoughts to herself and anything she said was to be taken as an order. When she mused through the ideas as she was doing now, on the other hand, she was open to Knave's thoughts and suggestions.

"So I'm thinking," she continued, "if the people we don't like are harassing our friends, it's only natural for us to come to the defense of our friends, right?"

Knave nodded his agreement, already recognizing where she was headed. "And if that assistance happens to reinforce our relationship with Triad, all the better."

"Precisely. It'd be like two birds with one stone." She grinned. "And we both know how much I love birds."

"Not exactly." When she raised a questioning eyebrow at him, he explained. "It would be more like three birds. We get to do some damage to the Iron Gauntlet," he spat out the name the same level of vehemence he would have done with a bite of rotten food, "we reinforce our relationship with the Qadar, and we get to show Triad that we're all friends here."

Diamond shot to her feet, her emerald eyes shining with excitement. "It gets even better, though."

"How could that possibly get any better? You've been wanting to increase your relationship with Triad for ages now and this is a perfect opportunity."

She nodded, brown curls bouncing against her cheeks as she did. "But now we get to take a shot against the Interplanetary Government, too!"

"Wait," Knave's brows lowered over all three eyes. "What are you talking about? Since when are we against the Interplanetary Government? Is that something we really want to take on?"

"I may or may not have intercepted a transmission a little while ago," she answered coyly. "That transmission didn't outright say much of anything but it strongly hinted that the Voivode Council had requested Triad's aid to help with the dual Iron Gauntlet and A.T. threat."

"Yeah, that makes sense. If I was in their position, I'd probably ask for Triad to come help too."

She nodded again. "But that's the thing, don't you see? Haven't you been paying attention?" She walked over to one of their viewscreen panels and activated it, clicking on the screen until the desired display appeared. "This is the Onoquoi system as it stands today. Here and here," she motioned to two groups of ships just outside the system's borders, "are A.T. and Iron Gauntlet ships, respectively."

"We knew that," Knave said, thoroughly confused on why she was showing him his own monitoring display. "That's why they called for reinforcements." He pushed himself to his feet and walked over next to her. "This right here," he indicated another ship, one parked just inside the Onoquoi border, "is Triad."

"Exactly." She looked up at him in triumph as though that somehow proved her point and explained her position.

He blinked between her and the viewscreen, trying to follow, to no avail. "They asked for help. Triad sent help. I'm not sure what you're getting at beyond that."

Diamond sighed and pursed her lips into a pout. "Oh come on, you're not being fun today at all."

"Sorry," he said amicably, "but I don't see

how Triad helping their allies gives us a reason to move against the Interplanetary Government."

"One ship." She didn't even look at the screen as she tapped it. "They sent one ship when there are so many more ships just beyond the system. Why would Triad only send one ship, particularly when A.T. is involved?"

Knave tilted his head to the side and examined the screen more closely. She had made a good point, he had to admit. For Triad to send only one warship, even one as advanced as the Stingray, was almost unheard-of. "Okay. So why did they only send one ship?"

"Because they didn't send the Stingray to defend Onoquoi."

Just when he thought he had caught up with her reasoning, she lost him again. "One more time, please?"

"The transmission I mentioned. It was a request for assistance. The Voivode Council expressly asked the Interplanetary Government to send Triad to help them. They were told no, that Triad wouldn't be deployed there."

Knave's face twisted in confusion. "Why would they refuse to send Triad? That kind of stuff is what Triad's made for, isn't it? Particularly when A.T. is involved."

Diamond nodded again. "Precisely. Because of that, you know Commander Moore's got to be pretty upset over this, they've been allies for longer than the Interplanetary Government's been around. Now being told to stand down when their allies are being threatened? When their assistance has been expressly requested and they're being told they can't come to their aid? Heck no." She grinned. "They bent the rules a bit. They were forbidden from sending support troops to help out but there's no rules against sending supplies, now is there?"

"And no rules about what kind of ship sends those supplies," Knave finally grasped what she had been getting at. "I get it. You think that there's some sort of feud among the Qadar, Triad, and the Interplanetary Government that stopped Triad from being deployed."

"Precisely. So all we need to do is go out and get in the way of the Iron Gauntlet, cause as much trouble for them as we can. By doing that, we help the Qadar, help Triad, and stick it to the Interplanetary Government, Iron Gauntlet, and even A.T. All without any of them knowing what the heck we're up to or why we're doing it." She looked thoughtful for a moment. "Well, there's one person who'll know what we're up to. I just hope he appreciates it."

"Do we have any idea why everyone's so intent on assaulting the Onoquoi system? I mean, there's resources there, sure, but nothing too special. Why are they so focused on it?"

"I have no idea," Diamond called over her shoulder, already halfway down the hall. "But I'm excited to find out. Whatever it is that they're after, if they want it so badly, then so do I!"

# EXPERIMENTAL PROCEDURE

"Where did you get all of these? Some of them aren't even available on the market yet!" Dr. Aditi was amazed at the sheer quantity of medical technology Jeoh had available in his lab. "Is that a neuropath chaser? I've been on the waiting list to get one of those for five years now." He moved from machine to machine, examining the ones he was familiar with to ensure they were fully operational and assessing the ones he wasn't to determine their function.

"You will find," Jeoh said as he pulled a bank of lights closer to the operating table, "that I have a great many things that aren't readily available on the open market. But if you insist on examining every piece of equipment, this will take far too long. Time is something we have in short supply." He turned on the lights and then looked over at M'Tarl. "Are you ready?"

"Wait just a moment," Dr. Aditi interjected as M'Tarl moved toward the table. "You aren't doing this procedure on her, are you?"

"Of course, why else do you think you have been brought here?"

"But..." Dr. Aditi stammered, "this is an unauthorized, experimental procedure. I had thought I was being brought here to oversee its testing, not to oversee it being tested on a humanoid." He looked from Jeoh to M'Tarl. "How are you okay with this?"

Jeoh answered before she had a chance to

speak up. "I have already completed the tests; everything will be fine. You are here because Triad personnel are overly cautious."

"But this is madness," the doctor continued to object. When it became apparent that nobody was listening to his concerns, he sighed. "Fine. If you're determined to go through with this, then I'll do my best to keep you alive during the process."

M'Tarl wouldn't just be lying on the table, sedated and unconscious, during the procedure as she had expected. Or rather, given Jeoh's previous inquiry about her pain tolerance, as she had hoped. Instead, she was placed in a seated position, the surprisingly comfortable adjustable table fully supporting her body once Jeoh was happy with her placement.

"There are a lot of similarities among humanoids," Jeoh explained when Dr. Aditi questioned why M'Tarl was being strapped securely to the table with thick leather bindings. "Not only are there obvious physiological similarities, such as quantity of appendages and such, many of the internal structures of the brain are similar among humanoid races as well. As a doctor who treats multiple races, I assume you are already well aware of this fact."

"I am," he agreed, "but that still doesn't answer why…"

Jeoh stopped him with a single glance as he secured a buckle. "Then I expect you also know about the brain-body barrier?"

"Yes," Dr. Aditi agreed. "It's a safeguard so that toxins entering the bloodstream elsewhere in the body don't infect the brain as well. It keeps the blood flow from one area localized to itself and reduces the probability of trauma and infections to the brain."

"Precisely. This compound is specifically designed to affect M'Tarl's psionic abilities, abilities that are housed within the brain. Because of that barrier, a simple intravenous injection in her arm or any other easily accessible blood vessel will do no good. It will never reach where it needs to go." He finished securing the last of the clamps around M'Tarl's head. "Comfortable?"

"About as comfortable as I suppose I'll be during all this," she agreed. "Really, I'm okay." She directed the last comment toward the concerned doctor. Although she was no longer able to turn her head to face him, she turned her eyes as far as she could in the hopes of making eye contact. "Besides, there's no way Gazer and her team will allow anything to happen to me while I'm here like this."

"We'll do our best," Gazer's voice came over the intercom. Since she and her team wouldn't be needed for the procedure itself, they were monitoring the progress through a series of live-feed video screens in the next room. M'Tarl would have been more comfortable had they been in the room but the sterile environment was critical and the fewer onlookers in person, the cleaner the room could remain. She had just finished recovering from the infections caused by receiving the damage so she wasn't overly eager to have new infections introduced during the restoration.

"That still doesn't explain why..." Dr. Aditi's

voice trailed off as realization set in. "You're injecting this straight into her brain?"

Jeoh nodded. "Thanks to the brain scans you so recently took of her we know precisely where the targeted areas are. That decreases the risks considerably."

"How do you know which spot to inject it into? We haven't fully worked out precisely which areas were affected by the damage. If you end up putting it into the wrong place, her powers will still be blocked and you'll have introduced the risk of infection for nothing."

"That is why I will be administering the compound to a number of locations. Fifteen, to be precise. At first, I had believed the compound would need to be injected into more than thirty places but my testing has decreased that number significantly. This will result in each section of her brain that may be the problematic zone containing an equal amount of the compound at all times."

He stepped away from M'Tarl and to a low table that held the rest of his equipment. "Any fewer and I cannot be assured that her powers will be returned. Where I tested with a larger amount in fewer locations, it quickly caused fatality. Any more is unnecessary risk, as you just mentioned. Injecting directly into fifteen sites is the safest option for her survival. Additionally, the injection sites will be very small as the needles are about half the diameter of a hair. That minimizes the open brain area and the risk of infection from that."

"For you to have done all that testing to find out how many sites you need to inject this stuff into," M'Tarl pointed out, eyes narrowing at his admission, "you would have to have created clones of my brain, not just an assortment of tissues." Had her head not been secured to the table, she would have turned to glare at him.

"Correct. Brain tissue is still tissue, after all. I never said which types of tissues I cloned. You should be pleased that I had the foresight to do all of the testing on clones of your brain tissue. I would hate to only discover once we've reached this point that there was a potential for catastrophic failure that hadn't been accounted for."

Despite her assurances to the contrary, M'Tarl was far from comfortable. Being restrained by a self-admitted mad scientist was uncomfortable at the very best, not only physically but mentally as well. This was easily the most vulnerable position she could imagine ever being in and the fact that she had done so willingly was already a decision she hoped to not regret. To make matters just that much worse, she needed to be awake for the entire thing so that her psionic abilities could be evaluated and assessed along the way, giving Jeoh the information he needed to adjust the dosage. The very last thing she wanted was to become the recipient of that catastrophic failure he had just so blithely mentioned.

As the first needle slipped through skin and into bone, she gritted her teeth. She had no preconceptions that having needles pressed through her scalp and skull to penetrate her brain would be pain-free, but it turned out to be so much worse than she had anticipated.

It was easily the most painful thing she had experienced, including the torture from which she still bore a handful of faint scars. The second needle was equally painful to the first, the third substantially more so. By the fourth needle, she was whimpering in pain. The only thing that kept her from reflexively flinching away from the injections was the series of straps keeping her restrained. She was howling in pain by the sixth needle.

The worst part was knowing that he wasn't even halfway done inserting them.

Rationally, she knew that the brain lacked pain receptors and, at Dr. Aditi's insistence, a local anesthetic had been administered at each of the injection sites. Despite all that, there was still a tremendous amount of pressure inside her head from all of the needles. Even though she knew she wasn't experiencing real pain, white-hot agony blossomed everywhere despite her knowledge. That pain wasn't just constrained to her brain, as it traveled down the length of her body, reaching every cell of her existence and causing all of them to scream in a chorus of anguish.

Jeoh, her most hated nemesis at that moment in time, the one who had talked her into the procedure, likely for the sole purpose of causing all of her suffering, did nothing to alleviate her distress. When she could no longer hold back a scream, he looked down at her, no concern whatsoever in his features, and had the gall to ask, "Did that hurt?" as though there was any doubt.

Unlike Jeoh's unemotional response, Dr. Aditi paled at M'Tarl's reaction. "Let's increase the anesthetic dose," he suggested, a comment Jeoh ignored. He reached around Jeoh's fast-moving hands to put more of the pain reliever on the most sensitive areas.

Even though she recognized that the effort was futile, as did everyone else in the room, M'Tarl appreciated his concern. "I'm okay," she panted between screams. "Are we almost done?"

"Closer," Jeoh said. "I've got the first couple

of sites penetrated, only a few more to go and then we can start adjusting the dosage."

M'Tarl blinked back tears at his words, a losing battle as she felt the first droplets roll down her face. Since she was unable to move, they were wiped away by the gentle hands of Dr. Aditi. Torture, she could handle. She'd been tortured a few times in her life. This, on the other hand, was different.

This was a whole new level of torment.

Twice she lost consciousness. Both times, she was revived almost immediately by a shot administered by Jeoh. "You need to stay awake," he reminded her. "I will not be able to tell when we've succeeded in this if you are not conscious." He smiled at her. "Unless you want me to check psionically. You can sleep if you just let me take a quick peek inside."

"Nice try," she retorted between gasps of air. Whatever he had injected her with felt like fire coursing through her veins, almost as painful as the needles in her skull were. A symphony of pain joined the agonizing chorus that had already spread throughout her body.

"But there's not a single chance in hell that I'll ever agree to that."

"As you wish," he agreed and stuck another needle into her brain.

After what felt like two years but was likely closer to forty-five minutes, she felt something begin to loosen in her head. The numbing sensation that had dulled all of her senses, particularly those she relied upon the most, began to let up. The pain that had coursed through her body since the ordeal began spiked immediately as every pain receptor flared anew, causing her vision to turn white and then black as consciousness tried to flee once more. As her power unleashed from the stranglehold that had held it in place, she reached out to detect the people in the room. Finding that easy enough to do, she expanded her reach further to explore deeper into the asteroid. Dr. Aditi was the only person in the asteroid who was not psionically protected and she was able to hear his thoughts loud and clear. "I think we've got it," she gasped finally.

"I think you're correct," Jeoh agreed. "You

sure you don't want anything else while I'm in here?"

"Certainly not. Get those things out of my head and get me off of this table."

Under the watchful eyes of Gazer and Dr. Aditi, Jeoh began removing the needles from her head. With each removal, M'Tarl breathed a sigh of relief as the pain eased. Once they were all removed and set aside, he sealed the injection points once again. Finally done, he released her restraints and caught her as she slipped from the table toward the floor, her fight to remain conscious finally over.

# IN GOOD STANDING

It took almost a month after the procedure for M'Tarl to fully heal and regain the complete use of her psionics. While she recovered, she spent her time in Jeoh's asteroid, wandering through the labyrinth of laboratories, storage areas, surprisingly comfortable living spaces, and banks upon banks of computer servers. Considering how much investigation and analysis he did on every creature he encountered, it would have been more surprising had he not possessed that level of computer equipment. But by and large, she spent the majority of her time on the comms, discussing and negotiating with the Voivode Council.

"We cannot restore you to your previous position until we have confirmation that you have returned to your previous power levels," Shuja Caolan said for the umpteenth time. "You are every bit as aware of this restriction as I am."

"Just to be clear," M'Tarl responded, "once I confirm that my powers are back, I will have my job again, is this correct?"

"We will need official documentation of that, of course."

"Of course. I assume that a medical record from Midway General should suffice."

"That is correct. Once we have that on file, there should be no further issues."

*That had better be enough*, M'Tarl thought to herself as she ended the call. That was all it had taken for her position to be taken away, so its return should be every bit as easy. The fact that it had taken so long, so many calls and so much negotiation for her to even be considered for return wasn't lost on her. Just why were they so eager to keep her away from the council? She hadn't gotten any sort of indication that there was anything against her personally and her record was stellar, so she had no clue why the Voivode Council was so reticent to reinstate her. She couldn't hold Shuja responsible for the delay in restoring her position but he was the only contact she had so he was the only target of her ire.

Well, Shuja and about a hundred clones of Jeoh. How did he manage to maintain so many copies of himself? Not for the first time, she wondered just how many of him there were. Just because she had only seen a few dozen at any given time, that didn't mean that was all there were. There were entire rooms, deep within his asteroid home, that contained nothing more than darkened clone pods. She'd never quite managed to see inside any of them to determine whether any were filled but she suspected that the majority, if not all, of them contained dormant clones. Working with Jeoh was very much like dealing with ants. Where there was one you could see, there were likely to be a hundred or so more just hiding out of sight.

"Any luck?" As though he knew he had entered her thoughts once more, Jeoh stepped into the room, a pair of steaming mugs in his hand. They contained one of his favorite beverages, a spicy mixture that tasted strongly of apples and nutmeg. Before meeting him, M'Tarl had never had the drink before but she had quickly grown a taste for it.

"Some, not much." She accepted the offered cup. "I will need to go to the hospital to get a full workup before they reinstate me."

"Easy enough. You are almost back to where your records indicate you should be, so the checkup is just a formality at this point."

"But I'm not quite there," she grumbled into her cup. "I had thought this whole thing would go much faster once everything unlocked."

"The worst of it is over," he reassured her

again. "Your power levels are already far in excess of your reported level two. The only reason it's taking longer than anyone expected is because you lied on your level readings."

She redirected her scowl from the steaming mug to his smug face. "You know you're not helping, don't you?" She sighed. "Thanks again for helping me get this far and for letting me stay here while I recover."

"No problem at all. It benefitted me just as much, if not more, as it benefitted you."

She raised a questioning brow at him. "How did it benefit you? Just by letting you get off this rock for a bit, or were the samples I collected actually something valuable?"

"No, and no. I have other places to which I can travel besides here, so that was only a small portion of it. And the samples you gathered for me, while new to my collection, were nothing extraordinary."

"Then how did any of this benefit you?"

"It allowed me to fully map the neural pathways of another sentient being. Until that point, I had only been able to experiment with copies of my own brain, so seeing how much of a difference there was between my brain and the brain of a Qadar was tremendously beneficial. The fact that you are also a psionist was simply an added bonus to all of that."

She should have known. In his eyes, she was nothing more than another experimental subject. That idea probably should have bothered her a lot more than it did but she had long since gotten used to his unusual viewpoint on things, herself included. She quietly turned back to her cup.

"I do have a question," Jeoh interrupted the silence. "Why are you in such a hurry to get back into the Voivode Council? Seems to me that there are lots of other ways for you to go about your business without them. Is it some sort of home world loyalty?"

"No, nothing like that." Her scowl faded as she sighed. "With them, I was doing important work, not just for them but for the Interplanetary Government as well. Now, I guess I just feel like the things I do won't have as big of an impact."

He harumphed into his own beverage at her words. "It's your choice, of course, but it seems to me that the loyalty you and your people have been showing to the Interplanetary Government hasn't been as two-directional as you'd expected."

"That's Shuja's concern, not mine. What I'm really after is the Iron Gauntlet."

He nodded. "I had thought it was something like that. Looking to get a little payback for what they've done to you?"

Her brows lowered as she examined her cup. "Not just that. I'm not sure if you'd heard, but they moved to attack Onoquoi recently. And that was on top of the fact that A.T. has been menacing us for a long time. Anything I can do to minimize one or the other of these threats, I am more than willing to do. A.T. is still a bit out of my league but I expect to be able to put quite a wrench into the Iron Gauntlet once I'm back in action."

"It appears that you have some company in that," he said as he gestured toward her notes. "Friend of yours?"

"Not exactly." She had been surprised when a mysterious force had arrived in the disputed area around Onoquoi, causing a tremendous disruption to both the Iron Gauntlet and to A.T., and had investigated as best she could from her secluded location. Without a whole lot to go on, she had developed a suspicion that she knew the source of the disruption. The only people she knew of who could get into and out of places, even ships like the ones under attack, as quickly and effectively as what she had witnessed were the Deck. If she had to place a wager, she'd bet on the Queen herself. "Someone else with a grudge against them, I think. It's just entertaining to watch, even if I'm not out in the middle of it."

Jeoh watched her silently for a long moment before turning to leave. Not for the first time, M'Tarl wondered how much more the man knew than what he was telling. There was something about his mannerisms, his demeanor, that led her to think that he knew something, perhaps even something important, about A.T., the Iron Gauntlet, or perhaps even both. Recognizing that and doing some-thing about it were two completely separate things, however, as he wasn't prone to sharing his knowledge and she had already learned quite well that prying information out of him, particularly if it was information he wasn't interested in sharing, was all but impossible.

The console before her flashed, indicating an incoming call. She answered, surprised to see none other than Shuja Caolan on the other end. "Did something happen?" she asked.

"You might say that. I just got off the comm with the Interplanetary Government, trying to find a way to get you restored to your position as I had promised."

She nodded. "I'm planning to go get that checkup in about a week or so, that should satisfy their requirements."

"No need. They have agreed to reinstate you on a temporary basis, effective immediately. If you agree, you will be fully restored to your previous position."

"What's the catch?"

"Two of them, actually. First of all, you

must be willing to submit to a full workup by a medical team of their choosing within one month. Since you said you planned on doing this anyway in about a week, I expect that won't be too much of a problem for you."

"Not at all. And the second catch?"

"They want you assigned to the Iron Gauntlet. Since they were your latest mission and you're believed to be dead, they feel you have the best chance of gathering further intelligence for us."

"I can easily agree to that, as I had planned on requesting this assignment anyway. But you are aware that the Iron Gauntlet knows I'm not dead, correct? Their assassins have already come after me a couple times since they supposedly killed me." She debated for a moment on mentioning her suspicions about those who were harassing the Iron Gauntlet and A.T. but decided against it. The less she explained now, the less she had to defend against later. Plus, her suspicions were just that: suspicions, not something she was in the habit of reporting about.

"I know. I got your report and the Interplanetary Government should have been aware of that as well. I don't know what their miscommunication involving you is about, but it seems like you're about to get your wish. I'd like to get your reinstatement underway before they realize their mistake and withdraw their authorization. Do you agree to these terms?"

M'Tarl blinked at the screen for a long moment before answering, her mind filled with questions, questions to which there was no good answer. Was it really going to be that simple? There had to be some reason why Shuja seemed to be so hurried. Was he really just exploiting a loophole? Finally she nodded, deciding that her questions could wait until later. "I agree to these terms."

Now, at the very least, she could go and get the answers she needed for herself.

The adventure continues in

**Wrecking Crew**

Available in 2027

Keep reading for an exclusive sneak peek!

Bright lights caused Buzzkill to wince even through her closed eyelids. She raised a hand to cover her face, hoping to block out at least some of the glare and felt a tugging sensation on her arm as it moved. She was lying down on something firm but reasonably soft, that much she could tell without any visual assistance, but anything more than that was a mystery to her. Gingerly, she cracked an eye and examined her surroundings.

As her eyes slowly and grudgingly focused, she realized that the lights weren't as bright as she had initially thought but the room itself was quite dim. That darkness had simply created a lot more contrast with the light that had woken her, making the illuminated area seem that much brighter. She blinked to clear the mental and visual fogginess and tried to figure out where she was.

She was on a bed with a pair of metallic rails pulled up on either side of her to keep her from accidentally falling off. To her left, a small table sat with a well-used notepad and a pair of pencils, one of which appeared to have been thoroughly chewed upon. Beyond the table was a window, through which she could see a clear night sky with a single cotton ball cloud floating past. No stars twinkled beyond the cloud, which meant she was in a much larger and more brightly-lit area. A bench covered in hideous green upholstery rested below the window with a closet completing that wall of the room. She examined her reflection, at least what little she could see of it, in the window to assess the damage.

Her hair, light brown speckled with the first hints of grey, was still short. She kept it above shoulder level, just to keep it out of her way. There wasn't quite enough light in the room to see her steel grey eyes, but she was reasonably certain that they were both there; missing eyes wouldn't cause quite so many visual issues. She could look down at herself and confirm that all five and a half feet of her was still present and accounted for beneath the thin blanket. Just past her feet, beyond the railing that marked the end of the bed, a door leading to a hallway stood slightly ajar.

The light from beyond the door was what had originally blinded her, the sterile white lights of a hospital, complete with the collection of antiseptic smells that normally accompanied any trip to such a facility. She groaned as the last pieces of the mental puzzle slipped into place and she realized where she must be.

The reason her arm had resisted movement to cover her face, she discovered, had been due to the pair of tubes leading into her right forearm, dripping liquids from two clear bags hanging from hooks above and slightly behind her head. One of the liquids was clear and from the label she could tell it was saline to keep her from dehydrating. She was well acquainted with that particular solution. The other liquid was a pale yellow, not one she recognized, and the label faced unhelpfully away from her.

As she blinked silently at the monitors to her right, half-heartedly wondering whether any of them indicated whether or not she was dying, the door opened further on silent hinges and a middle-aged man in powdery blue scrubs walked into the room. To his credit, he didn't turn on the overhead light, instead relying on the glow from beyond the door.

"Morning, Patient X," he said as he pulled a clipboard from the foot of her bed and flipped a page. "How are we feeling today?"

"Morning, Goober," she answered. "Is it morning? Still looks pretty dark out there." Dr. Goober had been the same doctor she had seen the last few times she had blown herself up, so it came as no surprise that he was the one in charge of treating her now. Although he knew that everyone called her Buzzkill, it was a rule for any physician treating a member of Triad, the intergalactic military, to maintain a level of anonymity. It was because of that anonymity that every Triad member treated at Midway General was referred to as Patient X. Or Patient Y. Or really any other patient name that consisted of a single letter.

"Early," he nodded as he flipped another page. "Very early. But your numbers are looking much better and you're even awake now, which is always a promising start, so let's take a closer look." He hooked the clipboard back on the foot of her bed and stepped around to her right.

He performed all of the usual checks, shining a small penlight into her already-sensitive eyes, checking her reflexes, and pressing across her abdomen to see how her internal organs felt. "Good news is that it doesn't look like you've got any lasting damage but I'm a little worried about your eyes," he said when she flinched from the lights again. I'd like to send you up for more scans and see how that brain of yours is healing."

Buzzkill rubbed a temple and nodded her agreement. "Assuming there's still a working brain in there, how bad are the rest of the damages?"

"You had some broken bones," Goober admitted. "Left humerus and clavicle. You hyperextended your left elbow so there was a little bit of tendon damage in there to heal up. You also cracked a few ribs and took a hell of a hit to the pelvis. But below that, everything's looking pretty good."

She was expecting the broken humerus, this wasn't the first time she had broken the upper bone in her arm, it was practically a routine injury for her by now. The clavicle wasn't altogether surprising either, since it was pretty well connected to the humerus. Broken ribs were almost a constant in her line of work so it would have been even more surprising had she not broken at least one or two of them. The fact that her lower body had taken virtually no damage was surprising, though. She glanced down the length of her body and wiggled her feet, just to confirm to herself that they did indeed still work. "What about my team?"

"Patient Y is in surgery, everything's looking good so far, and Patient Z is having another piece of metal welded on. What's the last thing you remember?"

"No surprise there. I swear, that boy's going to be a full-on cyborg if given half a chance. I, umm..." her voice trailed off as she realized she had no memories of how she had gotten to the hospital. "I was fighting, I know that much. We had a warship inbound and Glitch had me locked onto it, but I don't remember even firing a cannon."

While it may have seemed unusual for a patient to be talking to their doctor about fighting against warships, it had been many years since Buzzkill had been accused of being an average person. She piloted a Ragnarok, one of the largest mechanized units in her quadrant of the galaxy. Most of the people she encountered could hardly believe a single person could manage such a vehicle, particularly where the hectic field of battle was concerned. That disbelief was compounded by the fact that she'd never even known of the existence of mecha until a mere handful of years previously. She had taken to piloting mecha like the proverbial duck to water and once she had a target in her sights, nothing was going to stop her from eliminating it. Even accepting that her mecha could throw far more power at a target than could almost any terrestrial vehicle, using a mecha against a warship, even a small one, was almost unheard-of.

Unless, of course, one was to factor in the Wrecking Crew.

The Wrecking Crew was the team of specialized mecha pilots that Buzzkill led. There had been a handful of team members over the years, but the three who had been on the team with her from the beginning and were still active members were herself, her best friend Glitch, and Legion, who they weren't entirely certain still qualified as human. Her team was routinely sent to some of the most dangerous active hotspots where they repeatedly earned their name by wrecking anything that was in their way. Collateral damage was almost an expectation as far as they were concerned, if someone or something didn't know enough to get out of the way when they saw the Wrecking Crew coming, it was their own damn fault when they got a nasty case of hurt.

There were a few exceptions to that rule, but a warship wasn't among them.

"That's pretty normal," Goober assured her. "You took a hell of a hit and it's actually pretty normal to not remember traumatic events.

From the state you were in when you arrived, I'd have to say you definitely got into something pretty traumatic."

"Nothing new there. Traumatic is practically in the job description. I can't access the video feed from the server," she shook her head, wincing slightly in pain at the movement. "I've got my regular memories but when I try to check the upload history, I'm just getting static."

"Hm." Goober leaned in closer and moved the hair behind her right ear aside to view the access port for her neural interface implant. "I'm not seeing any damage here," he said after a quick investigation, "but I'll order a quick scan of that while we're poking around in your head."

Data was supposed to be automatically uploaded from the neural interface, commonly referred to as a brain jack, to her team's server every five minutes. While Buzzkill could tell that there was data available for the time between when she had activated the brain jack just before battle to when it had automatically powered down upon her arrival at the hospital, she was unable to access any of it. Her biggest concern was that there was some sort of damage to the electronics. "Might want to check the retinal implant too. Everything still looks way too bright and visual movement is kinda painful."

The brain jack wasn't just to upload battle data, although the data it gathered had proven invaluable time and time again in determining which tactics to use in each of their battles. The original intent of the device had been to allow Buzzkill to use her mecha in the first place. The sheer amount of firepower she used, the size of her machine, and all of the targeting systems were virtually impossible to effectively use without one. Between the neural interface and the retinal implant, which displayed data in real time for Buzzkill to read and respond to, she would be almost completely useless the next time she and her team were deployed.

"We can take a look," Goober agreed.

An hour later, Buzzkill was back in her

room to recover from all of the scans. They had found no brain damage, which was always a good thing in her opinion. Her retinal implant appeared to be functional as well, but they had found a minor issue with her brain jack which could have been causing the retinal interference. The repairs had been reasonably simple and fast to perform, so as soon as it was recharged, she could access the server again. Until then, she could at least see without pain.

Thankfully her room came with fast-charge capability, so what normally would have taken almost an hour on a standard port only took about fifteen minutes before everything could be powered on again. Once she was able to access the information, the circumstances that had landed her in the hospital made perfect sense.

She and her team had been planet-side, as usual, when the warship had breached airspace. Luckily, it was only a Mako-class warship, the smallest of the warships found in the galaxy. Not that it mattered, of course.

When considering warships, even the smallest of them dwarfed just about anything else in the sky or on the planet. By the time anyone had gotten a lock on the ship, it was breaching atmosphere, no small feat for a craft that size.

"Target locked on," Glitch's vocal recording said.

"Got 'im," Buzzkill responded. As the war-ship strafed towards them, firing deep plasma-filled trenches into the ground, she fired.

It had been obvious that the ship was trying to pull up and leave atmosphere again before Buzzkill's rounds made contact but anything that large was about as maneuverable as a red-wood tree. The Ragnarok's main cannon blew a crater in the lower front portion of the war-ship and removed any possibility of control. From that moment on, the result was both in-evitable and unavoidable.

While Buzzkill's colossal mecha was pos-itively tiny in comparison to the immense warship, causing it to be a smaller and thus more difficult target for the space-capable ve-hicle to hit, it's hard to miss when you throw something the size of a few football fields at a machine that stood slightly taller than a four-story building.

"Good thing I have that much armor," she said as she winced from the last image on her video feed before visual cut out, indicating the point at which she lost consciousness. "I guess I can cross getting into a head-on collision with a spaceship off of my bucket list." At the rate she was going, she realized, there wouldn't be much left that she hadn't already crossed off of that list. It seemed like she added another new experience on an almost daily basis.

She just wished that so many of them didn't hurt so badly afterwards.

Once she was done reviewing the footage and running a full system diagnostic on her implant network, she went to check on Glitch and Legion. Glitch, whom Goober had referred to as Patient Y, had been in surgery when she woke but he had been moved to a recovery room while she had been getting the neural interface repaired. Out of surgery he may have been, but conscious he definitely was not. She knew he was sleeping even before entering his room, as the loud snoring could attest. Deciding to let him rest, she went to check on Legion.

Both of Legion's eyes had long since been replaced with cybernetic ones, almost half of his head was covered in silvery plating, and the access port on his right arm sat open. His left hand held a small screwdriver, which he was using to make some adjustments in his open arm. His enormous and mostly metallic frame almost filled the standard-size bed he rested upon, and Buzzkill was impressed with the stamina of the frame to hold that much weight. He looked up as Buzzkill walked into the room. "I see you're alive."

Before he had started his collection of cybernetics, Legion had stood just under six feet tall and none of his new parts had changed that. He had lost a lot of his mass in other ways, however, as the requirements for biological versus mechanical sustainment had changed, causing his diet to change drastically along with them. Although Buzzkill knew that he had once been slightly obese, there was no longer any hint of anything other than lean muscle and metal now. Eventually, she was positive, the metal would win and no flesh would remain. To that end, he was already well along his way. But then, maybe that had been his goal from the first cybernetic upgrade he had received.

There was no emotion on his face, unsurprising considering how little face was there with which to emote. His blank expression, particularly when coupled with his disregard for social niceties, tended to put off most of the people he met but she was unfazed. She had long since grown used to his mannerisms. "Goober said you got more metal. What did you get this time?"

Rather than answering verbally, he tugged the sheet covering the lower half of his body aside to reveal a shining new cybernetic right foot. Just above the ankle, the skin was still red and raw, showing where the amputation had taken place.

"Necessary or elective?"

"Both," he answered as he turned back to tinkering in his arm. "It could have been saved but I'd need some physical therapy to get back into working order again. Having it replaced would need the same amount of healing time and it would be a lot easier to fix the next time I break it." He glanced back up at her before adding, "I wouldn't have to do the physical therapy for this, either."

"Probably not a bad plan. I was considering getting my ribs plated, too. Breaking them hurts like a mother, and healing takes forever." Unlike the man in the bed, the only cybernetics she had gotten so far were the neural interface and retinal implant. She hadn't really felt much need to go as overboard as her teammate. Given the recovery time for broken bones, however, she could understand his point of view. "What happened to your arm?"

"Just a slight adjustment to grip strength." He gestured with the screwdriver towards a bedside table. "I broke another pen."

Pens had been the bane of Legion's existence since he had gotten both hands replaced two years previously. Either his grip strength was too low to maintain hold of anything or he broke everything he touched. The pen in particular had proven to be an effective, if messy, test of both mobility and grip strength.

Since Legion hadn't engaged in small talk in over five years, Buzzkill wasn't going to press him to do so now, so she left him to his screwdriver. He seemed like he was fine, so she still had another team member to check in on. The snoring sounds had stopped, which she hoped was a positive sign.

"Perfect timing," Goober met her at Glitch's door. "He woke up a few minutes ago and I just finished my tests. You can go in and see him now but he's going to be tired so don't stay too long."

She didn't need the reminder, but she didn't bother saying as much to the doctor. He had probably just made the comment out of habit, but she and her team had been treated in these rooms more often than even she was certain of. Instead, she nodded and walked into the room.

Glitch was far paler than she had ever seen her olive-skinned friend. He had a couple days' worth of dark brown stubble across the lower half of his face, which did nothing to make him appear less ashen. His chocolate brown eyes were open slightly but watching her as she walked across the room and took a seat at his side. "How are you feeling?"

He shrugged in response. "Doctors say I've got brain damage."

"We've known that for years," she chuckled in response.

Instead of answering, he just grunted. Glitch had developed a problem with his synapses, causing the wrong information to get sent around his brain on occasion. So far this hadn't caused any substantial issues for him, except for an occasional misuse of language as he had difficulty selecting the correct words to use for the ideas he tried to convey. His speech issues were less troublesome than they were amusing, so the damage had not been enough to remove him from duty.

One effect stemming from the damage was

for his call sign to be changed to Glitch, which the entire team approved of. Just to be sure he wasn't saying he had new damage, she picked up his chart and began to flip through it. She didn't see anything alarming, so she settled the chart back into its position.

"Glad you're okay," he said finally. "I was a little worried."

"Nah," she laughed it off. "Gonna take more than a Mako to take me down."

"I tried to get to you," he looked at her sadly. "I knew it was coming at you and I wanted to get you out of there, but I was too far away." He scowled at his blanket. "I should have stayed closer."

"That's your job," she reminded him. "You did what you needed to do, so did I. We both made it out okay. No harm, no foul. Besides," she chuckled, "there wasn't anything you could have done. Even if you had gotten to me, you would've just been crushed, and probably wouldn't have survived."

They both knew that everything she was saying was true, but it was equally obvious that Glitch was feeling responsible for having targeted the warship. It didn't matter that his mecha was built with substantially less armor than hers was. It also didn't matter that she would have fired on the ship with or without his targeting assistance.

"Guess what Legion got." Buzzkill decided that changing the topic would probably have a better effect on her friend's mental state.

"Umm... lungs?"

"Nope. Kinda surprised he hasn't done that yet, but no. Try again." She let him guess a couple more times before explaining about Legion's new foot.

"Why'd he just get one?" Glitch wondered. "Should've gotten two. Matched set. Now he's gonna walk in spindles."

Even that small amount of conversation seemed to be exhausting the man, so Buzzkill told him to get some sleep and returned to her room to rest as well. For having been unconscious for the last few days, she was surprisingly tired as well. "Haven't I already slept enough?" she wondered to nobody in particular.

After life growing up in the beautifully rainy Pacific Northwest, Shanon L. Mayer tends to keep indoors, writing story after story, building vivid worlds on paper while her thoughts hold everything but images. She tends to look at everything in her world for inspiration – especially her collections of skulls, dragon statues, swords and knives, and pretty much anything that fits her eclectic, geeky-gothic lifestyle.

When her busy life feels like too much, she can be found relaxing with a hot mug of tea and a documentary on anything from theoretical physics to deep ocean wildlife to the most famous heists the world has ever seen.

www.ingramcontent.com/pod-product-compliance
Lightning Source LLC
Chambersburg PA
CBHW051429190726
48289CB00001B/115